The spider

by

Maria Savva

Published by:
Rose and Freedom Books
P.O. Box 55285
London N22 9EU
England, U.K.

A catalogue record of this book is available from the British Library

ISBN: 978-0-9928345-3-1

Acknowledgements:

Thank you to my fantastic editor Bob Helle, and my wonderful beta readers Darcia Helle, Jenny Hilborne, and Julie Elizabeth Aldridge for all your help and the valuable suggestions, corrections, and comments.

Thanks to my brilliant cover designer Kat McCarthy of Aeternum Designs for the awesome cover.

Thanks to my readers for your continued support.

Chapter One

'Can you kill it, Daddy? Please?' Four-year-old Robbie, with his Batman duvet pulled up close to his chin, squirmed, keeping his focus on the spider as he sat up in bed.

'It's only a spider, Robbie. Don't be scared, silly,' said George.

The creature, no more than about a centimetre in diameter, crawled along the carpet next to where George stood by the bedroom door.

'Let me pick it up and put it in the garden.'

'But it might climb back in through the window,' protested Robbie, wrinkling his tiny nose. 'Quick, Daddy! Kill it before it gets away!'

George smiled and rolled his eyes. He stomped on the spider a couple of times and then rubbed his slippered foot along the pile of the carpet to make sure he'd killed it, watching as the pieces of spider dissolved leaving a fine grey residue.

'Thanks, Daddy.'

Robbie's wide grin was reward enough for George, who quickly stopped feeling guilty about killing the innocent arachnid.

'Lie down, Robbie,' he said, tucking the child's duvet and blanket under the mattress on both sides of the bed. 'Time to sleep.'

George exited the room, switching off the bedroom light but leaving the door slightly ajar as the boy feared the dark and liked the hall light to be left on.

On entering the bathroom, George greeted his wife, Roisin, who was brushing her teeth. She nodded at him through the bathroom mirror, her mouth full of toothpaste. After spitting it out, she turned to face him. 'Did you read Robbie a story?'

'Yes.'

'Great. Is he asleep?'

'He was drifting off, then he saw a spider and shot up as if he'd seen a ghost. Nearly gave me a heart attack. I ended up having to kill it before he'd settle.'

'So, he's asleep now?'

'I don't know—'

'You should have waited with him until he fell asleep; you know how funny he is these days. He'll probably come to our room tonight. Remember last week, the trouble we had getting him back to bed?' She wiped her mouth with a face towel.

'All kids go through these phases, honey. He's most likely asleep by now, anyway. He was quite tired.'

'Yeah, he was out playing with that Liam from next door, on his bike.' Roisin frowned at the memory.

George squeezed toothpaste onto his brush.

'I'm not sure I like him playing with that boy,' she added.

'Why not?'

'He's older... How old is he? About eight?'

'So?' Some toothpaste escaped onto George's shirt as he uttered the word with a mouth full of foam.

'Well, he's quite a bit older.'

George spat into the sink. 'I know, but he's a good kid. Seems quiet. Likes playing on his bike and so does Robbie. Better he has someone to ride with than going out on his own.'

Roisin shrugged. 'Yeah, maybe you're right. I suppose I'm just judging the boy by his parents. That's not fair really, is it?'

'No—imagine if people judged Robbie by the way we behave! He'd never find anyone to play with.'

They both laughed.

'Anyway,' George quizzed, 'what's wrong with Liam's parents? I thought his dad was a doctor of some kind.'

'He's one of those PhD types. He's not a medical doctor.'

'He's called Hugh, isn't he?'

'Yes.'

'I've only spoken to him a couple of times. Seems okay, but then again we didn't talk for long.'

'It's not him I have a problem with, to be honest—I hardly ever see him—it's his wife who bothers me. She never smiles. I've tried speaking to her, you know, when I'm taking Robbie to school and collecting him. I have to walk past their house. I've tried walking with her to the school—I mean, the boys do go to the same school—but she's... I dunno... just not interested in talking to me.'

'She might be shy or not much of a people person.'

'No, it's not that, because I've seen her talking to some of the other parents: laughing and joking with them.'

Wiping his mouth, George glanced at his wife. 'I've only spoken to her a couple of times. She did seem a bit stuck up, I suppose. I remember asking if she and Hugh wanted to go to the pub with us, when they first moved next door. She reacted like I'd sworn at her. She said, "Hugh and I have plans tonight".' He mimicked her high-pitched, posh accent. 'She said they didn't like pubs and preferred a bottle of wine at home.'

'I get the impression she doesn't like Liam playing with Robbie,' said Roisin, folding her arms.

'She probably doesn't, but you've just said you don't either, so what's your point?'

Roisin let out an extended sigh.

'Let's go to bed,' said George. 'If the boys want to play together, I don't see any harm in it.' He walked towards the bathroom door.

'I don't like the way she acts like she's better than us, that's all. I don't want Robbie to start feeling inferior or anything because of the things she says.'

'He's only playing out with her lad, not going to his house, Roisin.'

'Yeah, but if they keep playing together he's gonna eventually want to go to his house, isn't he?'

'We'll cross that bridge when we come to it.'

Exiting the bathroom, they saw Robbie emerge from his bedroom rubbing his eyes.

'Robbie, get back to bed,' chided Roisin.

'Mummy, I can't sleep. Can I sleep in your bed?'

'No, darling, come on, back to bed.'

The boy began to cry. 'I'm not going back in there.' He sniffled. 'The other spiders are coming because Daddy killed their friend and they're going to try to kill us. We have to go to your room.' The tears flowed freely from Robbie's eyes and he ran towards Roisin, wrapping his arms around her legs.

She sighed and whispered to George, 'Why did you have to kill it? You could have taken it outside. You've upset him.'

'He asked me to kill it—'

'He's four years old,' she grumbled.

'Sorry,' said George.

The three of them trundled into the master bedroom and settled down to sleep.

Chapter Two

Abigail set the table as she did every evening, the food invariably cooked and ready at the same time. 7 p.m. Hugh often arrived home late and this would cause a subtle rage to boil inside her; by the time he got home she'd only be able to sneer at him by way of a welcome as he placidly kissed her cheek and asked, 'How was your day?'

She suspected Hugh was having an affair with the neighbour. Roisin. Abigail couldn't stand the woman. She imagined Roisin encouraged her son, Robbie, to start playing with Liam, in an attempt to find out more about the family, maybe gain Liam's trust. The nerve of the woman. What did she want? To replace her? Steal her husband and her son? Abigail knew that if she didn't do something soon—nip the boys' friendship in the bud—Liam would be asking if he could visit Robbie's house, then God only knew what schemes Roisin was devising. Round and round, these types of thoughts swirled through Abigail's mind, convinced as she was of her neighbour's double-dealing.

Sometimes—if she stopped long enough to think things through—Abigail felt foolish for doubting her husband's fidelity; there was no reason to suspect him.

Abigail met Hugh later in life. She'd been thirty-five and he'd been forty. She knew he'd had a previous relationship that lasted nearly ten years and that the girl broke his heart; she'd gathered that from conversations between his friends when they thought she wasn't listening. Abigail had seen photographs of Madeleine, his former fiancée: a pretty woman, her hair was the same natural blonde as Roisin's, her eyes the same crystal-clear blue. Abigail noticed the way Hugh looked at Roisin when they first introduced themselves to the neighbours. His eyes had locked into the young woman's eyes a bit longer than necessary, and he'd held her hand after the initial handshake for a good few seconds.

Since that first meeting, Abigail did everything possible to avoid the neighbours, and in particular to make sure Hugh and Roisin were not given the opportunity to get to know each other. The jealousy lived inside her like a bitter twisted thorn.

Whenever she saw Roisin on the school run, insecurity would rise to the surface. It made her regret the move to the neighbourhood. She constantly complained to Hugh, saying they'd made a mistake moving there and should consider selling up and relocating. Hugh liked the area, though, and said the school had an excellent reputation.

Abigail began to treat Hugh with contempt and this created a chasm between them. There was no intimacy. She knew she only had herself to blame, but her habits became increasingly difficult to break.

Today, Hugh arrived home at 7.05 p.m. and was about to kiss Abigail's cheek when she blurted out: 'Why are you late?'

Her abrupt question made him flinch. 'Wh-what's for dinner?' he asked.

'Stew,' she replied bluntly. 'We always have stew on Tuesdays. God, you've got a crap memory. I was just about to throw yours away.'

He lowered his eyes and took a seat at the kitchen table. In truth, he'd have preferred to sit on the side nearest the window, but Abigail had chosen it as her seat and no one else was allowed to sit there.

'Is Liam asleep?' he asked.

'No, he's doing his homework. I've told him to go to bed by eight.' She sprinkled some pepper on her food, then continued to eat.

Silence ensued for a few minutes as the couple ate. It wasn't a comfortable silence that might be expected after ten years of marriage. It was a silence fuelled by regret and disappointment. The atmosphere was heavy with the energy of hundreds of unspoken words, of conversations that would never take place; the words resided instead in an undercurrent of bitterness. Hugh would have liked to speak about his day, but lately his attempts at conversation had been received with rolling of eyes and exaggerated yawns. Abigail had never been interested in his work and recently she'd made no effort to pretend otherwise.

'Shall we put the telly on?' he asked as he normally did after the quiescence became overwhelming.

'You know I don't like having the TV on when we're eating, but you always put it on anyway. Why break the habit of a lifetime?' she said, rolling her eyes.

'If you were ever in the mood to talk, and not so snappy all the time, maybe I wouldn't have to put the TV on.'

'Snappy? If I'm snappy, maybe you have to ask yourself what you've done to cause that.'

'Me?' Hugh took a deep breath, trying to control his agitation. It wouldn't do to have a row now; Abigail never forgave him for losing his temper and found untold ways to punish him. She'd complain about it for weeks, for months, making him feel like he'd committed a crime; or she'd make him pay by refusing to talk to him for weeks on end, or sleeping in a separate bed for months. Not that anything went on in their bedroom even when they were together.

He switched on the television, his jaw clenched, pondering—as he frequently did—how he'd ended up in this loveless marriage. For a long time now he'd lived like a visitor in his own home, as if he didn't belong there. Abigail controlled everything. She'd chosen the house, the decor, the furniture; she'd even upholstered the chairs in fabric of her choice, putting her stamp on their possessions like a cat marking its territory. Despite all of that, she'd been saying she wanted to move again. It didn't make sense. His main desire was a longing to be free. A move anywhere else with Abigail wouldn't be freedom but more of the same. Yet he couldn't leave Liam, and doubted she'd allow him to have custody, or even allow him to see the boy if they ever divorced.

His mind drifted momentarily to the life he'd lived before meeting Abigail, but he stopped himself; the memories were too painful to recall. They belonged in the past. There were things he'd prefer not to remember and some that hurt too much to remember, so they remained locked away.

Abigail had never got on with his family or his friends. She didn't like most of them. Consequently, they'd moved far away from any of them. Hugh now felt like an accessory in Abigail's life. His only escape was his work, and he found himself staying at his office later and later to avoid returning home to the tension and the bitter words that awaited him.

'Are you watching this rubbish?' said Abigail, her voice storming into his thoughts.

Hugh snapped back to the present and focussed on the television. A sit-com; not one of his favourites. 'Er... no, you can switch over if you like.'

She picked up the remote and flicked through the channels. 'Don't know why we even have to watch TV when we eat. It's so... grrrr.' She switched over to the news channel and dropped the remote onto the table, her face hot with anger.

'We don't have to watch it,' said Hugh meekly.

'Bloody hell, Hugh! You can be so annoying!'

He began to pick at his meal. 'I saw the neighbour as I was coming in today,' he said.

'Oh, so we're going to talk now?' sneered Abigail.

'I'm just—'

'I can't listen to you and have that noise coming from the TV at the same time, so make up your mind!'

Hugh shrugged.

Switching off the television, she let out an exasperated sigh, and said, 'Which one?'

'What?'

'You said you saw the neighbour,' she huffed.

'Er... George. Nice man.'

'What's nice about him?' Abigail screwed up her face.

'They seem like a nice couple,' said Hugh.

Abgail appeared perturbed by his statement. A frown settled on her brow.

Although he hadn't seen much of George, Hugh sometimes saw his wife, Roisin, when he returned from work as she stood outside her house calling her son indoors.

Hugh often wondered why Abigail had to be so sour-faced all the time. Roisin always said hello and had a smile to share, even when she might not have had the best of days. She said things like, 'Robbie's been a terror today,' or 'Why did I decide to have children, hey?' but usually followed with a giggle. Hugh had grown to quite like her and found himself looking forward to seeing her standing there, feeling an odd sense of loss on the days when he didn't see her. It was almost a guilty secret.

He continued, 'George said he'd asked you if we'd like to join them in the pub one evening, but you said we didn't like pubs.'

'That must have been ages ago.' She waved her hand to dismiss the comment. 'I can't even remember talking to him.'

'He did say it was a while back, around the time we moved in, but at least it shows they were making an effort to get to know us.'

'Probably wanted to get some gossip,' said Abigail. 'You know what their type are like.'

'What do you mean "their type"?'

'Oh, come on Hugh, they're chavs.'

'What? Like my family were chavs? Why did you marry me?'

'At least you got an education, tried to better yourself, which can hardly be said about most of your family, can it?'

Hugh closed his eyes briefly. 'You can be so bloody self-righteous and condescending at times, Abi.'

'I don't want to talk about your family, okay?' she spat out.

'No... that's the problem. You never want to talk about anything but yourself.'

Her eyes widened.

'We've been living here a year and we don't know the neighbours at all,' he complained. 'We should try to get to know them. I don't like pubs much either—'

'Well, there you go then; they're not the type of people we'd get on with, are they?' she said, standing up.

Hugh wondered, with a sense of melancholy, what type of people Abigail *would* get on with. 'Abi, why don't we invite George and Roisin for a meal?'

Abigail narrowed her eyes. '*Roisin* is it? How do you know her name?'

'I found out her name not long after we moved in; I'm sure I've mentioned it before. You must have too; I mean, you often see her on the way to school.'

'I've seen the way you look at her,' said Abigail.

Hugh felt his cheeks redden. 'Wh-when? I never look at her... Only ever seen her a few times outside her door when I get home from work.'

'When we first moved in,' she said, pausing, a quiver in

her chin. 'You think she's pretty, don't you?'

'Er... why are we even having this conversation? She's married and so am I. What difference would it make?'

Abigail lowered her eyes and stared at the table.

'I just think we should make more of an effort to get to know the neighbours, Abi, that's all.'

'Why? We'll be moving away from here soon.' Abigail's stern expression dared him to contradict her.

'No... No, we've had that conversation and the school is ideal for Liam. We can't move him when he's just settled in.'

She slid back onto her seat, exhaling loudly.

'Before we got married, I used to enjoy going out with friends,' he moaned, 'and I used to enjoy parties, and yes, even pubs, but because of how you are—'

'How I am?' she boomed.

Hugh sighed. 'Let me finish.'

'I'm not listening.' She stood and picked up her empty plate. 'Have you finished with that?'

His eyes followed where her finger pointed and he looked at the half-eaten meal. 'I'm not hungry. I've lost my appetite.' Standing up, he used all his willpower to remain calm. 'Hear me out,' he said in a louder voice than intended.

Abigail seemed to be taken aback by his outburst.

He gained an inch of confidence and declared, 'We're having a dinner party and we're going to invite the neighbours. Liam plays with their son; we should get to know them.'

'Huh!' She stomped over to the sink and almost threw her plate into it. 'Right, and who's cooking the food for this dinner party? I can tell you it won't be me.'

'I'll do it,' he said. 'I can cook, you know.'

She stood facing him, arms folded, red-faced. 'I don't like parties,' she hissed.

'Well, I do.' Feeling a few inches taller, he strutted past

her, wondering why he'd not spoken his mind earlier. Swivelling around to face her, he added, 'And I'll be inviting my parents and my brothers and some of my old friends. It's about time they met Liam properly. You've been making the rules for far too long.'

He stormed out of the kitchen before she could retaliate, afraid his resolve wouldn't hold. An air of freedom washed over him as he made his way up the stairs, and he felt proud of taking a stand at last.

Chapter Three

'You'll never guess what happened this morning when I was taking Robbie to school,' said Roisin.

George twisted the pasta on his fork and raised his eyes to look at her. 'What?'

'Abigail from next door actually spoke to me... Not only that, she invited us to a dinner party at their house on Sunday. Can you believe it?'

After swallowing his mouthful of pasta, George smiled and said, 'See? She hasn't got anything against you.'

'Hmm... I'm not so sure.' Roisin wrinkled her nose. 'I just think it's weird. Usually she blanks me or gives me a dirty look. She wasn't particularly friendly when she asked, either. It sounded more like an afterthought. She was walking Liam to school, and as we walked past them he mentioned to Robbie that they were having a party. I turned around and happened to catch Abigail's eye. Liam said, "Mum, can Robbie come to the party?" and she looked at me and said they're having a small get-together to meet a few of the neighbours. "Hugh's idea. Bring the boy along if you're free. It starts at one." I had to run to catch up to her and ask whether we'd be able to stay with Robbie, and she stared down her nose at me and said, "Come along with your husband. I must dash now." Then she practically ran off.'

'Hugh seems like a decent bloke,' said George. 'I bumped into him the other day. I mentioned about when I'd asked Abigail if they'd like to join us at the pub. Maybe that got them thinking about how antisocial they've been.'

'Maybe.' An image of the handsome neighbour popped into Roisin's mind and she found herself blushing. She'd exchanged a few words with him when he returned home from work in the evenings sometimes, as she often called Robbie in for dinner or to get ready for bed at that time. On occasion, she'd found herself pondering how Hugh had ended up with such a haughty wife and whether they were happily married or not.

'It is a bit weird that they're inviting neighbours over to get to know them after living here for nearly a year. Not sure I want to go,' said George, jolting Roisin from her musing.

'We have to go. Robbie and Liam play together,' she replied agitatedly.

'Okay. You take Robbie.'

'Now who's being antisocial?'

'They're not really my sort of people.'

'How do you know if you haven't taken time to get to know them?'

'I just know.'

'I'm not going alone. I find it uncomfortable being around Abigail. I still can't shake the feeling that I've done something to offend her. She's so cold towards me.'

'I don't think you've done anything to offend her.'

'That's just it, neither do I.'

'She might just not be very friendly.'

'She speaks to lots of the other parents in the playground. Seems to know quite a few of them.'

'Her kid's in a different class. She probably knows the parents of the kids in Liam's class. You know, some people are like that when they don't know someone. You might find that she'll be nicer to you when you've spent a bit of time with her.'

Chapter Four

On Sunday, George escaped to the local pub at midday; he lied to Roisin, saying he and Glen were meeting up with an old school friend, Jim, who'd flown over from Canada and was only in town for the weekend so this would be their one chance to see him.

'Are you sure you're not just trying to get out of going to this stupid dinner party?' Roisin had said, eyes narrowed.

'No... You can speak to Jim on the phone if you want.'

'No need.' Roisin waved him off with her hand. 'Go and enjoy yourself. I'll suffer on my own.'

Secretly, Roisin felt pleased George wasn't accompanying her to the neighbours' house, nervous as she was about seeing Hugh again. Ever since being invited to the party, she realised she had a bit of a crush on him, and that made her feel like a fool. It was like a schoolgirl crush; she blushed at every mention of his name. Somehow, her imagination had latched on to an image of Hugh and—as he was handsome in a movie star kind of way—she had fallen for him. Knowing he was unattainable added to the charm: at least she hoped that was all it was. Every time she thought of him, a fluttering sensation erupted in her heart. Her mind boggled at the strange effect he had on her. At least today George wouldn't witness her fawning.

In truth, George wasn't seeing an old friend, but meeting his best friend, Glen, and their mutual friends Jess and Tom at the local pub. Jess and Tom had been at university with them and ended up getting married. When he entered the pub, he saw his friends seated at the far table where they usually sat.

'Hi George,' called out Glen. 'Glad you could make it.'

George chuckled and glanced at his watch. 'Er... yeah, sorry; I had a bit of trouble leaving the house. Robbie was playing up, so I helped Roisin get him ready.'

'So what's this party you were desperate to avoid?' asked Tom.

Pulling a stool over to the table, George joined them. 'It's at the neighbours' house. They arranged a dinner party and invited us, but I'd rather pull my own teeth out with pliers than go to their house.'

Glen laughed. 'They can't be that bad.'

'Believe me, they are.' He looked at the table and noticed they hadn't bought any drinks. 'Have you ordered your lunch yet?'

'No, we were waiting for you,' said Tom.

After ordering their food, the four friends sat at the table with a round of drinks.

'So tell us more about these neighbours, George, I'm intrigued,' said Glen.

'Nothing to tell.' He took a sip of his beer. 'They're a bit too stuck-up, that's all; I don't think we have anything in common. They've lived next door for nearly a year and hardly spoken to us, and then suddenly they arrange a dinner party. Well, it's the woman who mostly ignores us; the husband is out working all the time.'

'Probably works late to avoid the missus,' joked Glen.

'Ha, ha! That wouldn't surprise me,' said George, raising an eyebrow.

'You might like them if you get to know them,' said Jess.

'I doubt it,' said George.

'So is Roisin all right about going on her own?' asked Jess.

'She said it'd be rude not to go. Robbie is friends with

their son.'

'I bet she was cursing you,' said Tom.

'I would be,' said Jess. 'Imagine sending her to meet the snooty neighbours on her own.'

'Don't listen to Miss Know-It-All.' Glen rolled his eyes. 'You did the right thing, mate.'

'"Know-It-All"? That's rich coming from you,' snarled Jess. 'You're always claiming to know everything.'

'Mirrors,' said Tom, nodding.

'What're you on about?' said Glen.

'We see reflections of ourselves in others. It's something I read somewhere.'

'Huh! You've been spending too long around Jess. Your brain's gone soft.'

'At least he has a brain,' Jess countered.

'Calm down, everyone,' said George.

The food was served, offering a welcome break from discussions.

'Where's your husband?' asked Abigail before she even said hello, peering past Roisin when she opened the front door. 'Is he on his way?'

She didn't make eye contact, and that put Roisin on edge slightly. 'Um... no, he's been called away: something important at work.'

'On a Sunday?' Abigail spun around, not staying to find out the answer.

Roisin stood on the doorstep unsure whether to follow her neighbour into the house or go back home. She was left with no alternative but to join the party when Robbie heard Liam's voice and let go of her hand, running into the hallway.

Feeling very out of place, Roisin closed the front door

behind her and stood still, not sure where Abigail had gone.

'Roisin, isn't it?' said a deep voice from the doorway of the living room.

It was Hugh.

Roisin noticed again how handsome he was. She'd never been this close to him before. He'd dressed very smartly for the dinner party. A fresh smell of aftershave drifted towards her as he reached out his hand to shake hers. His eyes were the most stunning green, like emeralds.

How did stuck-up Abigail end up married to this gorgeous man? She almost began to feel sorry for him, then she snapped out of her trance and told herself that he must be just as horrible as Abigail if they were husband and wife.

Gritting her teeth, she shook his hand. 'N-nice to finally meet you properly,' she said.

'Yes, definitely.' He looked at the front door. 'Are you on your own? Where's your husband?'

'Um... he had to go out.' Somehow she couldn't bring herself to lie so easily to Hugh; his demeanour was so much more welcoming than Abigail's.

'Can I get you a drink?' he asked.

'Yes... uh, orange juice. Thanks.'

'We can do better than that,' he said, winking at her. 'Shall I put a bit of vodka in it?' He made his way over to the bar in the living room.

As she watched him from the doorway, she recalled how she'd felt as a teenager whenever a boy had shown any interest in her. Her cheeks burned. She thought she'd left all those awkward feelings behind with her single status.

I love George, she reminded herself—then proceeded into the living room.

Hugh approached her with a smile and his gemstone eyes.

She took the proffered vodka and orange and drank it

down a bit too quickly.

'Shall I get you another?' he asked, raising his eyebrows.

She gawped at the empty plastic cup and said, 'I-I must have been thirstier than I thought.' Her cheeks were still hot, making her feel even more self-conscious.

'Don't worry, I'll get you a refill.' He took the cup and his hand brushed against hers as he did so.

She shivered, and goosebumps appeared on her arms. *Where's Robbie?* she wondered, determined to find him and make an excuse so they could leave early.

Abigail stormed into the room just as Hugh returned to Roisin's side with a second vodka and orange in his hand.

When Roisin looked at Abigail she saw her eyes were fixed in a piercing, almost accusatory stare.

The woman turned away when Roisin's eyes met hers. 'Hugh, you're needed in the kitchen.' Her voice was full of scorn.

'Of course, my love,' he answered. 'Excuse me,' he said to Roisin, handing over the plastic cup. He flashed a smile at his wife, who sighed in response and left the room.

Roisin was left alone in the living room in a state of confusion, a tornado of questions twisting through her mind: *Why* did Abigail seem to hate her so much? Had she done something to deserve such abrasive treatment? How could Hugh hold such power over her emotions? How could he reduce her to a bumbling mess with just one look? Round and round the questions went. She could find no answers.

'No one's ever come out of that house alive,' said George, swigging the last of his beer.

'That's ridiculous,' said Glen.

'No it isn't.' George placed his empty glass on the table in front of him. 'Last month, there was a story in the local paper about a homeless man who broke in and was never seen again.'

'Don't believe everything you read in the papers,' said Tom. 'Who's buying the next round?' he asked, holding up an empty pint glass.

'Your turn, cheapskate,' retorted Glen. 'You're not getting away with it like the last time, Tom-Tom.'

'I bought the last round,' said Jess. 'It's unfair that me and Tom have to both buy rounds when we're living on one income.'

'Stop whinging, Jess,' huffed Glen. 'Oh, all right then, I'll get the next round.'

'Mine's a Guinness,' said Tom. 'What about you, Jess?'

'I'm feeling quite full after that meal; I don't want anything else to drink,' she replied.

'Good, 'cause I don't wanna buy you anything,' said Glen.

Jess made a face at him.

When Glen had returned with the drinks, he said, 'George, what you were saying about the house in Goldfern Road? You don't believe it, do you?'

'Yeah, of course. People just go missing.'

'Okay, so a homeless man went missing, but homeless people are fairly isolated—alone most of the time. They don't know many people. He could still be out there, just that no one knows him.'

'No, no... Apparently, he used to go to a place once a week to get free food,' explained George, 'and every day he'd meet up with other homeless people in a shelter to pass the time. After he went into the house on Goldfern Road, no one saw him again.'

'There must be some explanation,' said Tom, taking a sip of his beer. 'People don't suddenly disappear into thin air.'

'They can. What about alien abductions?' mooted Glen. 'Or spontaneous combustion?'

'There's no proof that any of those exist,' said Tom.

'You insensitive prick,' thundered Glen. 'My nan spontaneously combusted right in front of my granddad and he's never been able to get over it. He's always worried that someone will burst into flames in front of him—has anxiety and everything.'

'Oh, my God, that's awful,' said Jess.

'Sorry, Glen. I didn't mean—' began Tom.

Glen laughed. 'You two are so gullible.'

'Bastard,' blurted Jess. 'That was cruel. You shouldn't joke about that kind of stuff.'

'You need to get a sense of humour, Jess.'

'You need to understand what's funny and what's not,' she grumbled. 'You wouldn't be laughing if your nan actually did spontaneously combust, would you?'

'Well, that's where you're wrong because I would find that quite funny,' said Glen, grinning.

'You're warped,' said Tom.

'It was only a joke. What's wrong with you two?'

'Anyway,' continued George. 'Back to the house on Goldfern Road. I'm as sceptical as the next person, but the history of the house can't be denied. It's been sitting empty for months. No one dares to go inside because of the stories.'

'So, a homeless man went missing,' said Glen, shrugging, 'what else happened?'

'A couple of months before that, some squatters moved in, but they disappeared... Never came out.'

'There could be like a serial killer who hates homeless people killing them off in there,' suggested Tom.

'No. No one lives there. A man used to live there alone, but after he left it stayed empty for some reason.'

'Maybe he died in the house and his ghost is haunting the place, killing people.'

'Ghosts don't exist, Tom,' said Glen. 'There's got to be another explanation.'

'I used to live in a haunted house,' said Jess.

'Oh, yeah, I remember you telling me.'

'Look, you two can carry on your ghost stories when you get home. It's all rubbish. We all know what your imagination is like, Jess.'

'What's that supposed to mean?' she scowled.

'You can get a bit carried away, that's all I'm saying.' Glen shrugged.

'It was haunted. It wasn't just me who—'

'Did you see a ghost in there?' interrupted Glen.

'No, but—'

'I rest my case.'

'There was a ghost.'

'Who cares?'

'Don't be so rude,' snapped Tom.

'Sorry Tom-Tom. I just want to find out more about this house where all the homeless people are being killed off. Tell us more, George.'

George shook his head. 'It's not only homeless people. Policemen went into the house and disappeared. They even sent in a priest to do an exorcism, but he never came out.'

'There must be someone in there who's killing these people or keeping them hostage,' said Glen.

'It's a neighbourhood watch area, apparently, and no one has heard anyone in there or seen anyone go in or out.'

'If he's a serial killer he wouldn't go out, would he? Least not in daytime hours when people can see him,' opined Tom.

'Why d'you keep saying "he"?' complained Jess. 'There have been plenty of serial killers who were women, y'know.'

'Yeah, I've had my suspicions about you for a while now, Jess.' Glen chuckled.

'Very funny.'

'Y'know, I reckon it's all old wives' tales,' said George.

'Might be old husbands' tales.' Glen sniggered and winked at Jess.

'You're so immature,' groaned Jess.

'Anyway, these kinds of things get blown out of proportion,' said George.

'Yeah, so would you go into the house?' asked Tom.

'Dunno.'

'That means you believe the stories.'

'What if it's like the Bermuda Triangle, y'know, where there are these weird pockets on Earth where people disappear.'

George dismissed the idea with a wave of his hand: 'Bermuda Triangle doesn't exist, Jess.'

'Isn't that a Barry Manilow song?' Glen laughed.

'Ha, ha! Yes,' said Tom.

The three men began to sing an out-of-tune version of the hit.

Jess covered her ears. 'Karaoke night is tomorrow.'

'So, when are we gonna check out this place?' asked Glen after a fit of giggles.

The others stopped laughing and stared blankly at him.

'What?' Glen held out his palms. 'These types of opportunities don't come around that often. Houses in Goldfern Road go for nearly a million quid. We could do it up and sell it on.'

'You'd never be able to sell a house with that kind of history.'

'Course I could, George. Once I've gone in there and

redecorated it, all the bullshit stories will be blown out of the water.'

'I'm not going in there,' said Jess.

'No one invited you.' Glen stuck out his tongue.

Jess ignored him.

'Listen,' said George, 'I think we should all go together, or not at all. That way, if there's any truth in it we'd have a better chance of escaping. We'll take knives with us.'

'You really serious about this?' Tom looked at him wide-eyed.

'I know a man who can get a gun,' whispered Glen.

They all stared at him.

'What?' He raised his eyebrows. 'We have to make sure we can defend ourselves, don't we?'

'H-how d'you know someone who can get a—' started George.

'Shhhh... Keep it down, mate, dunno if there's any coppers in here.'

'Huh! If there are, we can send them to Goldfern Road and get rid of 'em.' Tom chuckled.

'That's a valid point, actually,' said Jess. 'Police are armed, aren't they? If they didn't escape, how could we?'

'Not all police are armed,' said Glen. 'In fact, most of them aren't. Where do you get your information from, Jess?'

She gave him a searing look.

'There are special firearms units when they need to be armed,' interjected Tom.

'Yeah,' said Jess. 'If they were going in there to raid the place, they would've been armed, wouldn't they?'

'Whatever, I don't believe any coppers have been in there; it's all scaremongering,' snorted Glen.

'This is all too freaky for me, I'm out.' Tom stood up. 'C'mon Jess, we're leaving.'

George and Glen sat together after the couple had gone.

'You serious about doing this?' asked George.

'I wanna, but not sure.' Glen tapped his beer mat on the wooden table, then turned to his friend: 'Look, we can split the profits. I know some great builders who are cheap, and they'll do the place up in no time. We can sell it on and you'll get half. What d'you say?'

'We should try to find out more about the place.'

'You know how the news exaggerates everything, George. A homeless man goes missing, a group of squatters —those people live under the radar anyway; no one would know where they are. They prefer it that way. Probably wanted to go missing and escape some crime, so they used the house as a cover. Now all the superstitious nonsense stops people going there. It's an ideal investment opportunity.'

'Yeah, but what about the coppers that went missing, and the priest?' asked George, raising his eyebrows.

'Sounds like a load of baloney to me. Like something out of those *Hammer House of Horror* movies.' Glen shook his head. 'I bet it's all Chinese whispers. Rumours spread like wildfire among sheeple. The more absurd the rumour, the more people believe it. Human nature.'

'You're very philosophical today.' George laughed.

Glen smiled. 'Let's go and talk to some of the neighbours and ask, at least. We'll say we used to know the bloke who lived there and see whether they have a forwarding address for him—see what we can find out. Chances are he wants rid of the place and we can do a deal with him, get it cheap.'

Chapter Five

Walking along Goldfern Road, George took in the scenery. He'd hardly visited this part of town. The houses on this road were expensive, four-bedroomed, many of them semi-detached. Most of them had their own drives.

Number 8, the vacant house, was identical to its neighbours, except that the windows were boarded up. There was nothing sinister about its appearance.

'There it is,' said Glen as they stood outside the house. 'Our investment opportunity.'

'Hmm...' mumbled George.

'C'mon, let's see if the neighbours know anything about it.' Glen ran towards 6 Goldfern Road.

A young woman answered the door.

'Hello... uh, sorry to bother you,' said Glen, 'but we're from out of town. We used to know the man who lived next door. The house looks empty. D'you have any idea where he's moved to?' He smiled pleasantly at the young woman.

'No, sorry, I only moved in a few months ago. Thinking of moving again, though. Next door is pretty creepy. I'm sure I hear noises coming from there sometimes, but no one comes in or goes out and it kind of freaks me out. You should ask Theo, the neighbour on the other side of the house: number ten. He has some interesting stories about the house.' She frowned and ran a hand through her blonde hair. 'Theo's stories are part of the reason I'm thinking of moving on, actually.'

'Okay, thanks, we'll ask him.'

Glen and George made their way to 10 Goldfern Road.

'I don't like the sound of this,' said George. 'You sure you wanna go through with it? We can't sell a house we don't own, anyway. You heard what that lady said; she's freaked out by the place.'

'No offence, mate, but it didn't look like it would take a lot to freak her out.'

George chuckled. 'You can be such a misogynist at times.'

'You being rude?' Glen wrinkled his brow. 'What's a misogynist?'

'It means you hate women.'

'I don't hate them. Well, not all of 'em.'

'I thought you'd quite fancy that woman we just spoke to. Blondes are your type, right?'

'Yeah, but she was too skinny.'

'You can't be so picky; you'll never find anyone.'

'What, and end up happily married like you?'

'I am happily married.'

'Yeah, keep telling yourself that.'

'What is it with you and women?'

'What d'you mean?'

'You hate all your mates' wives and girlfriends. You're always being cruel to Jess.'

'She asks for it.'

'She's quite nice.'

'Yeah, if you like bimbos.' Glen sighed. 'Look, it's mutual; they hate me as much as I hate them. It's cool.'

'You just haven't met the right one yet.'

'Oh, and you have?'

'Yeah, actually. Roisin's my soulmate.'

'Pardon me while I puke.'

'She doesn't like you much, either. Says you're a bad influence.'

They arrived at 10 Goldfern Road, and Glen rang the doorbell. 'She's probably right,' he said, glaring at George.

The door opened and there stood an elderly man of

Mediterranean appearance with a balding head. 'How can I help you, gentlemen?' His accent was foreign.

'You're Theo, right?' said Glen.

'It depends whether you want to know or if the police do.' The old man chuckled. 'Yes, yes, I'm Theo.'

'Your neighbour at number six said you knew about the house next door. We were wondering where the man who lived there has moved to,' said Glen, smiling. 'We came to visit him—used to know him years ago—but it looks like he's moved.'

'Um... that must be Dave?' Theo elaborated: 'Dave lived there before the most recent owner, for many years.' Theo knitted his brow. 'You two don't seem old enough to have known him.'

'He was a friend of my mum's,' piped up Glen. 'I remember visiting him as a kid. I was hoping to be able to see him. But as he's moved, maybe we could have a look at the house, for old times' sake.'

'I wouldn't go into that house if I were you, son,' said Theo, looking them up and down as if he were attempting to gauge whether they were trustworthy. 'If you'd like to come in for a cup of tea, I'll explain what happened.'

Glen glanced at George, a self-satisfied smirk on his face. Then, addressing Theo, he said, 'Yes, thanks, that'd be great.'

They sat in the musty living room on a threadbare brown sofa next to a coffee table. The old man hobbled in carrying a silver tray, upon which sat three cups of tea and a plate of biscuits that appeared stale.

As he placed the tray on the table, he said, 'Sorry about the mess, boys; it's not the same here since my wife died. She was so good at cleaning the place. I'm useless.' The old man laughed.

The boys laughed along with him.

'Anyway, you want to know about the house next door, yes?'

'Yes, please,' said Glen.

George nodded.

'Dave moved out, must be just over a year ago. That's when everything changed. Have you not heard the stories in the news?'

'No, uh, we're from out of town,' said Glen.

'I see. Well, around here it's a famous house. Sometimes, I feel nervous living so close to it. There are all sorts of rumours. Some people say there's a murderer living there, but I don't see anyone coming or going, and I've never heard a sound from there. Okay, maybe sometimes at night when it's quiet it sounds like there might be something, but it's more like creaking floorboards—really creepy.'

'The neighbour on the other side said she's thinking of moving,' said George.

'Yes. Lisa. She's a lovely girl. She moved in with her boyfriend a few months ago, but they split up and now she lives there alone. She said she sometimes hears something moving in the house, but she hasn't noticed anyone go in or out, either.'

'Have you considered moving?' asked George.

'I wanted to when my wife died. I put the house on the market, but there was no interest. The estate agent said it was because of the recession, but to be honest, son, I think the reputation of the empty house next door puts people off.'

'In what way?' prompted Glen.

'People go missing.'

'What d'you mean?'

'I know it sounds strange,' said Theo. 'I used to be in and out of Dave's house—we were great friends—but I wouldn't set foot in that house today if you paid me a million pounds.'

'So how did it start?' asked George.

'The man who bought the house from Dave started decorating, well—more than that—he was changing things. There was lots of dust and noise, bricks everywhere, like he was knocking down walls. I found out he didn't have planning permission, so I complained to the council about the noise. It was a waste of time; they didn't do anything about it. After that we kind of fell out, so I didn't visit or talk to him.

'One day, Rex—that was his name—wasn't there anymore. I assumed he'd moved out, but no one else lived there and his car was still parked outside. Bailiffs came round because he hadn't paid his taxes. The two men who went in never came out. They'd broken the lock on the door to get in. Then a couple of squatters got in, young boys. Disappeared. Then, last month a homeless man went in... Same thing. A priest went in because some of the local residents thought it might be haunted and they asked him to, you know, what's the word—'

'What? To do an exorcism?' asked Glen.

'Yes, that's it. But he disappeared, too.'

'Weird,' said George.

'It's a mystery.' Theo nodded. 'Since then, no one dares to go in there. The police did watch the house for a while because they wanted to work out if someone is holding people hostage, but so far there's no news.'

'They can't just have disappeared. Doesn't make sense,' said Glen, his brow creased.

'I can't get my head round it.' Theo shrugged. 'I've sometimes thought about going in there myself, but somehow can't find the courage.'

'Why doesn't the council knock it down?' asked George.

'That's what we want. One of the neighbours has started a petition, and the police also want to get in there, but no one has decided the best plan. To be honest, I think they're all too scared. They don't know what's happening. And, let's be honest, it takes the police and council ages to get anything done. They're treating it like a bomb waiting to go off.'

'Surely, they could do one of those dawn raids with lots of officers,' said Glen.

'They were planning something like that, I think.' Theo rubbed his chin. 'It was supposed to happen not long after the priest disappeared, but it didn't go ahead. Something to do with health and safety rules.'

'Come to think of it, I heard a couple of police officers went missing in there,' said Glen.

'I thought you didn't know about the place,' queried Theo.

'Uh...' Glen looked at George, then back at Theo. 'I didn't, but what you said made me remember something I heard on the news.'

'Hmm...' Theo nodded. 'It wouldn't surprise me, but no I haven't heard about that. I'm sure the police would be taking it more seriously if they lost some officers in there.'

'Yes, that's true,' said Glen. He finished his tea and placed his cup in the tray. 'Thanks for taking the time to fill us in, Theo. We'll be off now.'

'Um... you came to see Dave, didn't you?' said the old man. 'I have his mobile number somewhere. I haven't kept in touch with him, I'm afraid. We were close friends, but after my wife died I kind of went into my shell for a while and wasn't up to seeing people. I was thinking about him the other day, actually. I know I have his number somewhere, but for the life of me I can't remember where.'

'Oh, don't worry,' said Glen.

'Look, give me your number and I'll call you when I find it.'

George and Glen gave Theo their numbers and left the house.

'You can't still be thinking of going in there, Glen; are you off your rocker?' George stared in incredulity at his friend as they sat across from each other in the local pub.

'This is a once-in-a-lifetime opportunity. How many times do you get the chance to buy a million-pound house for a fraction of the price and sell it on for a fortune?'

'You heard what Theo said: the police have their eye on the property, and the council want to knock it down. You'll never get to buy it, so forget it.'

'All those stories are a load of mumbo jumbo. As if the police and council would leave the property alone if all those things had actually happened. It's all rumours. If the police and council were onto it, they'd be looking for this Rex and asking him questions.'

'Okay, I have an idea; why don't we do a search for this Rex character on the Internet?'

'We don't know his full name. Shit, why didn't we think of asking Theo?'

'Let's just forget about it.'

'No,' said Glen. 'Wait! My sister-in-law is a solicitor. She could find out whose name is on the title of the property.'

Chapter Six

'I can't believe we're doing this,' said George, looking over at the house. In the half-light it conjured up images from old horror movies. He switched off the engine and took off his seat-belt.

'Yes, we are,' said Glen. 'It's going to be great. This time next year we'll be lying on an exotic beach without a care in the world. It's not every day opportunities like this come along, you know.'

'Yeah, you keep saying that, but I don't see why we have to go in there now. We haven't even traced the owner. He might not even agree to sell it to us.'

'That Rex bloke has gone AWOL. The only address for him on the property register was this one. We'll have to work out a way to claim ownership of the property: I'm sure there's a way of doing that if you move in and live there for a while. I read a story about a man recently who moved into a property when the owner died and did some repair work and treated it as his own. He got a judgment in court saying he could keep the property.'

'Oh yeah, I remember reading the story. Hadn't he been living there for years?'

'No, only a couple of years. Okay, he'd been treating it as his own for maybe ten years, but there must be loopholes we can find. I'm sure that if no one claims the house, it's ours.' Glen rubbed his hands together.

'Sounds too good to be true.'

'So, you up for it?'

'I don't think it'd work. Sorry.'

'Look, mate, I'm going in. If you're too lily-livered to join me, that's your problem. You won't get a share of the profits when I sell.'

George turned his attention back to the house. The road was quiet, eerily so. There was no one around, as though time had stood still. There was no sign of life at all. Then he watched as a leaf fell from a tree and slowly drifted on the wind towards the road, and a cat darted past the front gate of the house. His eyes drifted back to the windows, which appeared black in the dying light due to the boards that were placed there. It was uninviting, and he couldn't help thinking about the rumours of people disappearing inside as if it were some kind of black hole or portal to another world. 'I'm a dad,' he said. 'I have to think about Robbie. I don't want him growing up without a dad.'

'Think how much you'll be doing for him by getting half a million from the sale of this place. He'd be set up for life.'

'Give me a few days to think about it,' said George, taking another look at the ghostly house.

'No. It's now or never. You're either with me, or you lose.'

'But I'm supposed to be going to the neighbours' house with Roisin tonight. They invited us over because I wasn't able to go to their party with her last week.'

'What? When you escaped to the pub?'

'Yeah.'

'So why would you wanna go there now? I thought you hate them.'

'I do... Well, maybe *hate* is too strong a word, but I wouldn't want to spend an evening with them.'

'There you go, then. Phone Roisin and say something's come up.'

'But she was pissed off the last time when I didn't go to the party with her.'

'It'll work out for the best; this way she gets to cancel the arrangement... I mean, it was only arranged so you could

go along, wasn't it? Roisin'll probably thank you for it.'
     'That's a good point.'

Chapter Seven

'Wh-where are we?' Glen looked over at George, who was close by—he could tell by his breathing and a thrashing about as he tried to move, but he couldn't see him. It was dark, apart from a small crack of light entering through a brick; some kind of ventilation hole.

'I can't move,' said George, sounding panicked. 'Shit, Glen, what've you got us into?'

'Blame me—'

'Who the fuck else is there to blame?' George shifted slightly. 'C-can you move?'

'I couldn't a minute ago, but after I came out of whatever that was, a blackout or something, I started getting some feeling back. I think we were drugged. I didn't see anyone though.' Glen tried pulling himself up, but there were handcuffs and chains on his arms, one of which seemed to be attached to the wall. 'Shit. Where are we?'

'We're in your million-pound house, you bloody idiot. If we get out alive I'm gonna kill you.'

'The last thing I remember was walking through the door.'

'You were saying how the place only needed a couple of coats of paint... then... then you started to fall, like you were fainting, and I called out to you, but then I felt really dizzy, and I blacked out.'

'Yeah, you're right, I remember that now.'

'It's so quiet. Do you think this is what happened to the other victims?'

'Shut up, George. We're not victims. You're freaking me out.'

'No one ever came out of here alive,' said George, morbidly.

'Oh my God, you're going to kill me with depressing thoughts before any serial killer has a chance.'

'I'm glad you find it funny. Maybe it's because you don't have a family to think about. You're so bloody selfish. Why did I listen to you?'

'Pull yourself together—' George's fear was contagious. Glen's bravado slipped away as dark thoughts bombarded him and he remembered what George had told him in the pub about all the people who'd gone into the house and were never seen again. In desperation, he tried tugging his left hand, which was attached to the wall by a handcuff, but the edge of the handcuff cut into his wrist, causing him to wince.

'Pull myself together? Pull myself together? We're in a house with a serial killer.'

'He won't kill us,' Glen said quickly, as if to reassure himself. His head was spinning as anxiety took hold.

'Yeah, so what happened to all those others? Does he like playing a prison warden? I have a bad feeling about all this, Glen.' George began to cry.

'Stop it,' pleaded Glen. The darkness felt like a vortex that threatened to engulf him.

'That's rich coming from you... This w-was y-y-your idea,' George said between sobs, 'and now I'm n-never gonna see m-my boy again. Never gonna get out of here!'

'You don't know that. We'll figure out a way—' He heard his heart beat in his ears, smothering the sound of his friend's sniffles.

Approaching footsteps sounded. Loud and heavy. A hinge creaked as the door to the room opened, letting in faded light.

A large figure stood silhouetted against the grey backdrop. Then the door closed again and the blackness resumed. The only slight light came through the vented

41

brick, trickling in from up above the dingy basement room.

'Well, well, well,' muttered a grizzly, crackly voice. 'What do we have here?'

'Wh-who are you?' ventured Glen.

'I could ask you two the same question,' growled the figure, who now appeared to be sitting on a chair—although it was hard to be sure in the dim light. 'What are you doing in my home? You're trespassing. I have the right to shoot you, you know... Well, I would have in certain states in America. This country is too soft on criminals.'

'What you're doing is criminal,' accused Glen.

'It's not. It's natural. I'm the spider, you are the flies who have flown into my web. I didn't go out and capture you. You came to my house.'

'Y-your house. So you're Rex?' asked Glen.

'First rule of a serial killer: never give away your identity,' mumbled the man before bursting into raucous laughter.

'A s-serial killer? So you *did* kill all of those people who came in...' George gulped.

'As if I would tell you if I had.'

'You can't kill me, I have a young son... He's only four. He needs me.'

'Pity I never took up the violin. It would have come in handy,' jibed the man.

He shifted position and both Glen and George squirmed and pulled back as far towards the wall as the chains allowed.

'Glen, you bastard, I'm gonna kill you,' whispered George.

'Um... I saw him first,' said the serial killer.

George began to sob.

'Stop crying you coward. Listen, if it makes you feel better I've never killed anyone.'

Both men let out audible sighs. 'S-so you'll let us go?' said Glen.

'I didn't say that. And when I said I've never killed anyone, I meant *yet*. I've not killed anyone *yet*. You are the final pieces to my puzzle. I can now set my plan in motion.' His words echoed in the empty room.

'What plan? W-we can help you; let us know what you want. We can give you money,' babbled Glen.

'I don't want your money, and I don't want your help. You've helped me enough already by walking into my trap. Spiders have eight legs. Eight eyes too, most of them. I made sure the house was numbered eight. Now I have my eight victims.'

'Wh-where are the others?' asked Glen.

'Each room is carefully soundproofed. You won't hear anything from them. Most of the time they're asleep.' He laughed, then continued, 'It's interesting how similar the number eight is to the infinity symbol; I'm sure it means that once my work is done, I will become immortal. All I have to do is add you to the web and my work here will be done.'

'Wh-what web?' asked Glen.

'As a boy, I was bitten by a spider,' the captor carried on as if he hadn't heard Glen speak. 'D'you know how upset I was when I didn't get any special powers? I didn't turn into Spiderman. All that happened was I had an allergic reaction and went to hospital. I wanted to become Spiderman. Just like in the film. But they lied. You don't get anything if you're bitten by a spider, only a bite.'

'Spiderman... well, Peter Parker was bitten by a radioactive spider, that's why he got powers,' said George.

'Are you trying to be clever?' The strange man's question echoed in the room.

'What the fuck, George,' whispered Glen. 'This is a madman, don't say anything.'

'Oh, I can assure you I'm not mad.'

Glen coughed. 'I—'

'Save your apologies,' boomed the grizzly voice. 'I know all too well that the spider that bit Mr Parker was a special spider, but I also know that I was meant to become Spiderman. It was supposed to happen in one way or another so I could use my powers to take over the world. I was disappointed that the spider bite was not effective. That's when I started watching spiders. I studied them. Some would say I became obsessed by them. If I could learn their secrets I could change my world, I felt sure of it. You know, I may not have become Spiderman when I was bitten, but I am convinced that the spider did give me something. He gave me a gift, an inner understanding of spiders and an insight into their world.'

George and Glen turned instinctively towards each other in the darkness.

'Spiders make a web and wait for their prey to become entangled in it,' the man elaborated. 'They don't kill them straight away, you know. They usually inject them with poison to liquefy them, and they wrap them in silk. It's very methodical and well thought out. My web is nearly complete. Six victims. They are all ready to take their places. Now you two make eight. The perfect number.' The man walked around the room as he spoke.

George winced each time he came close to him. 'Wh-what are you going to do to us?' he asked.

The man sat down. 'I have built a web. It's beautiful. It's not made of silk; that wouldn't have been strong enough to hold my prey. It's made of wood. Intricately carved to resemble a web. I'm very proud of it. My eight victims will look so magnificent on the web, wrapped in silk. The finest silk. I had it imported, and they told me it's made from actual spiderwebs. It cost a lot of money, so they'd better not have been lying to me. I will have my day. I will prove all those doubters wrong; I did get special powers when I was bitten by the spider. Something changed in me then. I became Spiderman. Not in a Hollywood super-hero type of way. I'm not out to save the world. Not the human world. I am a spider in a man's body. I am a real spider. The Spider. Now the world will have to sit up and listen. They will have to believe. My only regret is that it won't be those same people who used to taunt me who'll end up in my web.' He took a deep breath.

'M-maybe we can help you find them. If you tell us who they are, we'll go out there and get them for you, bring them here,' offered Glen.

The Spider remained silent, as if contemplating the offer. 'Hmm...' he began, 'Perhaps if you'd come earlier. I'm running out of food supplies down here, you know. I can't last much longer. Your arrival was perfect timing.'

'We can get food. We'll bring food back for you,' said George quickly.

'Yeah,' said Glen.

The Spider laughed. 'You actually think I'd let you out and give you the opportunity to get help? You'd ruin it all, wouldn't you? Humans ruin everything. Do you know how many innocent spiders are killed by humans? It's like some kind of sport. People go on about fox hunting and how inhumane it is. What about killing spiders? Huh? Huh?'

He paced the room. 'People don't think twice about killing a poor defenceless spider. The spider would perhaps be trying to find its way out of a house having become trapped, but a human will step on it. Cold blooded, that's what it is. What I'm doing is making a statement. I'm speaking for poor creatures who cannot speak for themselves. See how you like it now you've met a spider your own size. I won't let you win. You'll meet your fate on my web before the night is through.'

'Th-the police are planning to raid the house,' said Glen. 'It-it could be today; they'll find you.'

The man started to laugh. He laughed for a minute or so, a disturbing, ear-piercing sound.

'Police?' he said finally. 'No one enters this place without becoming a victim. I finally found a use for the top-secret formula that I researched whilst at university. I call it sleeping-spider gas. I had access to all sorts of chemicals and gases. I was a science graduate. I found the perfect combination of sleeping gas and other similar gases, combined with traces of venom from a very special kind of spider, which I think is a nice touch. It hasn't failed me yet. Whenever anyone walks into the house, the gassing system is activated.'

'Look, mate, I think you've done well,' started Glen.

'I'm not your mate. I am The Spider and you will address me as such.'

'Sorry.'

'You are trying to worm your way out of the chains that bind you, but it's too late. People have tried to laugh at me, belittle me, all my life. Never believing that I am supreme.'

'You've proved you're Spiderman,' said Glen. 'No one can laugh at you now. In fact, let us out and we'll tell the world that you're Spiderman, the best Spiderman, won't we, George?'

'Er... yeah, yeah we will.'

'We won't file charges against you; in fact, we'll say you looked after us, and we'll get the others to say the same.'

The man loomed over them. 'Be quiet. You are nothing but flies. Your words buzz around in my ears and they mean nothing. I'm done with this world. You are not listening to me. My time here is over. I have a higher purpose. This will be my grand finale. I will burn this place to the ground, but first I need to see my web in all its glory with the flies in their designated places. Then I'll finally know what a spider feels like. Then I will be one with them. All those who tried to tell me I had no power will be proved wrong. I will go down in history, like Guy Fawkes. Every year they will celebrate my day. I will be remembered. The Spider.'

He made his way to the door, his shadow momentarily covering the faded light that was seeping in through the cracks around it. Then the light switch was flicked and the room became visible.

The two friends had to close their eyes against the light.

'I will leave you here while I make the final preparations,' said the man.

He was dressed in a fur cloak that had long spindly protrusions, four on each side. Spider legs. The back of the costume was designed like the body of a huge spider.

When the man turned towards them, before leaving the room, they saw he'd blackened his face with some kind of paint and wore deely boppers on his head as antennae.

He left the room.

'Oh my fucking God,' said Glen, 'Who the... What the... Who the hell is that man?'

'I have no idea, but he's obviously off his head.'

'He's a fucking weirdo. All that Spiderman stuff and dressed like a spider. He's a freak.'

'He obviously has serious issues.'

'Yeah, well, there's no way I'm being killed by a freak dressed in the worst spider fancy dress costume in the world. We've gotta get out of here. You heard him; he's planning to burn the place down.'

'This has got to be some weird dream I'm having,' said

George. 'Are we still in the pub? Did you put any hallucinatory drugs in my beer?'

'Shut up and help me get these handcuffs off; there must be a way.'

George tugged as hard as he could, trying to free himself from the wall. 'We should both pull together.'

Glen leaned over and took hold of his friend's arm. They both pulled hard and the cement in the wall crumbled, loosening the brick.

'Yes!' said George.

'Keep your voice down. You don't want the psycho version of the Honey Monster coming back in, do you?'

'How can you joke at a time like this?'

'What do you want me to do, you freak? Cry?'

'Mayb—'

'Look, I'm as freaked out as you are, but there's no sense in both of us falling apart.'

'Falling apart? We could be burned to ashes in the next few hours, I think that's a good enough reason to panic.'

'Relax. We'll find a way out. Pull the chain, we need to get the other one out.'

They persisted in pulling together against the wall and eventually the brick holding the chain loosened and fell out.

They found their feet, wobbling slightly.

'My legs have gone to sleep,' said George, shaking his left foot.

'Have you seen these walls?' said Glen.

George looked up.

The whole room was painted with a spiderweb design; eerie cocoons depicted flies trapped in lace-like silk. 'This is too weird.'

They were still handcuffed together and had to carry the bricks with them as they were dangling from the chains that had been attached to the wall. 'Maybe we can whack him over the head with these bricks,' suggested Glen.

'Good thinking.'

'It's got to have an element of surprise. God knows what other chemicals he's got up there. He knocked us out with that sleeping gas. He's some kind of nutty professor. Anyway, as far as I know, he would have had to use something else to keep us out of action for long enough to bring us down here. He must've injected us with a drug.' Glen lifted his arm with some effort due to the weight of the brick. 'Yeah, there's blood, and it's bruised.'

George frowned. 'He must be a psycho.'

'Duh! Have you just figured that out?'

'Shh...' George swivelled his eyes from side to side. 'Can you hear that?'

'I think it's our furry friend upstairs.'

'We'll have to try and get out.'

'He's probably locked the door,' said Glen, pulling at the handcuff so George would follow.

'Are we gonna risk it?'

'Do we have a choice? I don't want to end up being barbecued by a freak, do you?'

'No.'

'Follow me.'

'Yeah, as if I can do anything else,' said George, holding up his wrist and the handcuffs that kept the two men bound together.

Chapter Eight

Roisin approached the neighbours' front door. She hoped Abigail would answer it, then she could make an excuse about George being unable to make it. If Hugh opened the door and invited her in, she doubted she'd be able to resist.

Over the past week, since the dinner party, her thoughts drifted to Hugh every time she had a moment to herself. She'd find herself contemplating the colour of the leaves on the trees, as she gazed out of the window whilst washing the dishes, and comparing them to Hugh's eyes. Other times, she imagined Hugh lying beside her in bed instead of George, and then felt terribly guilty when the idea turned her on.

What made it worse was her awareness that it was a mutual attraction. Hugh had hardly taken his eyes off her at the party, and he'd been the one who'd invited her back for dinner.

As Roisin stepped out of the house after the party the week before, Abigail held the front door open, appearing impatient for her to leave.

'Bye, thanks for coming,' Hugh had said.

Abigail gave her a disparaging look and got ready to close the door as soon as Roisin and Robbie were outside.

'Pity your husband wasn't able to make it,' Hugh continued. 'Listen, why don't you both come over next Sunday? We'll have a nice dinner.'

Abigail's mouth fell open at the suggestion. 'We'll have to check our diary, Hugh,' she'd said, trying to catch his eye.

He said, 'We'd love to have you,' not even acknowledging Abigail.

Roisin blushed.

'Next Sunday at seven o'clock,' he'd insisted, 'we'll be

looking forward to it.'

Abigail's cheeks were a fiery red.

Roisin heard shouting emanating from within the house after the door had been closed. Once again, she was left wondering what she'd done to offend the woman.

A week later, Roisin stood outside the front door. She'd taken Robbie to her sister's house, and was cursing George. He was pushing her away. She'd expressed her anxiety about the way Abigail treated her and yet he'd not stood by her; instead, he'd called to say he couldn't make it—something about having to do overtime at work—but she could have sworn she heard Glen laughing in the background. He'd probably gone to the pub with Glen, preferring to spend time with his friends.

Trying to banish the negative thoughts, she rang the doorbell.

Hugh opened the door.

The early-evening sun shining and reflecting off the glass in the door, made it appear that there was a halo over his head. Roisin had to catch her breath before speaking.

'Hello,' she said, and couldn't help the smile that burst onto her face.

'Welcome. Come in.' Hugh gestured for her to enter with a wave of his hand, and his broad smile reflected her own.

She wanted to go inside, but stopped herself. 'Sorry, George can't make it, so we'll have to rearrange. I hope we haven't put you to too much trouble.'

Hugh's smile faded. 'Um... where's Robbie?'

'He's at my sister's house.'

'Good.' Some of the brightness returned to Hugh's face as he uttered the word. 'Look, Roisin, you'd be doing me a favour; I need someone to talk to. Abi's not here.'

'Where is she?'

'I'll explain.'

Roisin followed him pensively into the house, breathing in the fresh, sensual scent of his aftershave, recalling how his muscles had rippled when he flexed his arm to close the front door. *So toned. Not like George.*

Hugh ushered her into the living room and went over to the bar at the far side of the room. Pouring himself a whisky, he turned towards her. 'What would you like to drink?'

'Um... just water, thanks.'

'I'll get you some wine, shall I?' He winked. 'Please take a seat.'

She did as he requested, as if hypnotised.

He handed her a full glass of white wine and slid down to sit next to her on the luxurious, white leather sofa.

'So, Roisin. That's an Irish name, isn't it?'

'Yes, my dad was Irish.'

'Was?'

'He died.'

'I'm sorry.'

'It was a long time ago.'

Silence followed.

'I should go,' she said, after taking a sip of wine. She'd warned her sister, Priscilla, it was possible she'd be coerced into staying for the meal, so she told her that she might have to look after Robbie for the evening. Priscilla had been happy to do so. Her two children loved playing with Robbie. Even so, Roisin was unable to shake a strange sense of foreboding: she gulped down the rest of her wine, feeling desperate to leave.

'Please stay,' said Hugh. 'Abi's taken Liam to her mother's house. It's a few miles away. She's gone for the week; God knows how she's going to get him to school every day. She doesn't think anything through. We had a row. I told her to leave him with me, but she says I'm a bad influence. Huh. She's the bad influence; a mother who's miserable all the time.' He tipped back his head and finished his whisky, then went to pour another.

Roisin saw him wobble slightly on standing up, and wondered if he might already be drunk.

'It's been a long time coming. She's been a real bitch for years and I have no idea why I've put up with it. No, actually, I probably put up with it for Liam's sake; but in hindsight Liam would be better off without all the disagreements and arguments we've had, and without all the bitterness following Abi around like a bad smell. I knew she was damaged goods when we got together—her last partner abused her—I stupidly thought I could help her, but she's cold as ice. Plus, I'm not sure whether I believe her about the abuse. She's pretty controlling and abusive herself.' He knocked back another whisky.

Not quite sure what to say or how to react, Roisin sat staring at Hugh. Then, when he looked at her as if expecting a response, she said, 'I'm sorry, I had no idea.'

He sat close to her on the sofa, and she could feel the heat from his arm.

'Your husband's pretty elusive.'

Roisin was not sure how to reply to that: *He's gone to the pub with his friend rather than spend the evening with you,* didn't strike her as appropriate.

Before she had the chance to respond, Hugh asked, 'What's your relationship like? You get on okay?'

'Yes,' she said, attempting to cover up any hints he might be getting about her attraction to him. 'We're a typical married couple, I suppose; we have our ups and downs.'

'More ups than downs, or downs than ups?' probed Hugh.

She blushed. As he leant towards her, she could smell the sweetness of the whisky on his warm breath.

Straightening her skirt, she shuffled away from him, trying not to make it too obvious that she was deliberately putting distance between them. 'We're just a normal married couple.' She felt sure her cheeks must be at least a deep crimson by now.

'I only ask because Abi and I haven't slept together for months.'

Roisin stared at him.

'Don't get me wrong, I don't think marriage is all about sex, but once in a blue moon would be nice. If I annoy Abi—and believe me, it doesn't take much to annoy her—she refuses to sleep with me for ages.' His eyes met hers.

Roisin averted her gaze.

'S-so why do you stay together if she—' She regretted asking the question but it was too late to retract it.

'Liam, I s'pose.'

Nodding, she stared at her hands.

'So, you and George, you're happy together?'

'Yes,' she replied, unable to meet his eyes.

'Really?' he asked, raising an eyebrow.

She caught his eye and gulped as he placed a hand on her knee.

Hugh leaned in and kissed her full on the lips.

Roisin thought of the past week and the times George had kissed her and she'd imagined it was Hugh. *Maybe that's what this is*, she thought, *it's my mind playing tricks on me... This can't be happening.*

Hugh pulled away and stood up. 'I'm sorry, I shouldn't have... I've met your husband outside a couple of times and he seems like a decent bloke. Please, let's forget it happened.'

'Okay.' She sensed a combination of relief and disappointment. *He's gorgeous*, she found herself thinking, despite tremendous guilt building up inside and images of Robbie and George cascading through her mind. The butterflies in her stomach were wishing Hugh would kiss her again. It would have to be his decision, though, not hers. She felt terrible about betraying George, but she hadn't been this attracted to anyone else for a long time.

She picked up her handbag and made to leave. Her legs wobbled and she questioned whether it was the wine or the way Hugh made her feel. 'Um... I'd better go.'

'Yes,' said Hugh.

They stood staring at each other.

'If you weren't married to... Never mind, it doesn't matter.' He went back to the bar to refill his glass. 'Stay and have another drink before you go, at least. I need some company.'

'Um... I don't know if that would be wise.'

'I promise I won't kiss you again.'

'That's the problem. I haven't been able to stop thinking about you since last week, and—' She stopped herself. *What am I saying?*

Hugh handed her the refilled wine glass, a glint in his eye. 'You feel the same?'

She caught her breath.

'Sit down, Roisin. We should talk about this.'

'Er... N-no, I think I should go.'

'If you were happy with your husband, you wouldn't be thinking of me, would you? If there's one thing I've learned from staying with Abi all these years, it's that you can't get the lost time back. The years of feeling miserable, feeling trapped. You have to make a change for your own sanity.'

He drank down the whisky and returned to the bar for a refill.

She began to suspect he may have a drink problem.

'Years with that cow have turned me into a nervous

wreck. If I had someone like you...' His eyes fixed on hers from across the room.

She stood holding her full wine glass. *Should I stay or go?* As the thought entered her head, so did the popular song by The Clash, *Should I Stay or Should I Go?*, and it was all she could do to stop herself singing the song. She had to suppress a desire to giggle, then worried that she'd already consumed too much wine.

She was locked into his stare for a moment. Pulling her eyes away, she drank the glass of wine in one go and sat back down on the sofa. Thoughts of George flooded her mind. *If he'd been here with me today, none of this would be happening. It's his own fault. He's always down the pub with Glen.*

Hugh sat next to her on the sofa. 'You're not happy, Roisin, are you?' Lifting a hand to stroke her cheek, he whispered, 'You wouldn't be sitting here drinking with me on a Sunday evening if you were happy in your marriage.'

His speech had become slightly slurred, she noticed. Looking directly at him, she said, 'I don't know... B-but an affair? I don't think I could do that to George.'

'If he cared, he'd be here now.' Hugh ran his fingers along her upper arm. 'Just like Abi, he's not here. It's only us; they've left us alone.'

He kissed her neck, making her shiver as he ran his hand down her back. When he kissed her lips she found herself kissing him back, and before she knew what was happening he'd taken off her blouse and skirt and she found herself lying on the sofa half-naked. His fresh-smelling aftershave intoxicated her senses, and she felt woozy from the wine. When he removed his trousers she wondered if she was doing the right thing, but the doubt crept into her conscience for the briefest of moments like a whisper blown away on the wind. It was wrong, but it felt so right.

He pulled her closer to him. 'Relax, Roisin, this will be

our secret. Your husband doesn't know how lucky he is to have you.'

An hour later, Roisin sat opposite Hugh at the kitchen table. Abigail's kitchen. Everything screamed Abigail, from the floral decor to the doilies on the table. Oddly, Roisin was feeling as though she'd just defeated a staunch opponent.

Hugh was sipping freshly brewed coffee from a mug emblazoned with the words "Best Husband in the World".

He chuckled as she eyed the mug. 'I chose this cup deliberately,' he said. 'I haven't drunk from it in about ten years. Abi bought it on our first wedding anniversary, probably as an afterthought on the day from the bargain bin at the local supermarket.'

Roisin smiled, feeling numb. When she'd read the words *Best Husband In The World,* she remembered how for a long time after they married, she'd often referred to George as the best husband in the world. Those had been happier times but, regardless, she knew that what she had just done was very wrong. George hadn't crossed her mind once while she was having sex with Hugh, on the sofa, then on the floor, then on his bed: the bed he shared with Abigail. The sheets were currently in the washer-dryer. She listened to the hum of the machine that would get rid of the evidence. She'd been confused by her emotions, imagined sex with Hugh might make her feel better. It hadn't.

'We have to do something about this,' said Hugh.

She cast aside her melancholy musings and raised an eyebrow. 'What d'you mean?'

'You and me. I've decided I'm divorcing Abi.'

Despite the inevitable guilt, Roisin felt happy. Happy. For the first time in a long while. An alien emotion. 'I thought I was happy with George,' she said speaking her mind.

'But you're not?'

'Evidently, I'm not.'

He took her hand from across the table. 'I think life's too short to be anything but happy.'

'I'm confused.'

'It's not your fault. It takes two to tango.'

'Um, Hugh, what happened today, I've never done anything like that. I've never cheated on anyone. It's wrong. I don't feel like I've done anything wrong, I don't feel dirty, but I should, shouldn't I?'

'You only followed your heart.'

'Yes, but I have a son to think about.' She had a sudden panic attack and glanced at her watch. 'Phew... it's not as late as I thought... I've lost track of time.'

'Stay a bit longer.'

'I have to go. I need to collect Robbie from my sister's; he's got school tomorrow. And George might be home by now.' She took her handbag from the back of the chair.

Hugh stood up to face her. 'I want you to know I didn't plan any of this. It just happened. But now it has, we have to do something; I don't want to wake up at the age of sixty and regret not taking this chance.'

She took his hand and said, 'Why isn't life straightforward?'

He kissed the top of her head. 'Abi's away this week, so please come and see me. I'm usually home by seven in the evening.'

'I need to be at home for Robbie.'

'Your husband can look after him. Make an excuse; say you're meeting a friend.'

'What? And pop over to the neighbour for sex while he's next door with my son? I don't think that would be the smartest move.'

'But... But we can go somewhere else, I can meet you

—,'

'Where? In a sleazy hotel room, checked in as Mr and Mrs Smith?'

'No.'

'Look, Hugh, we shouldn't have done this; it must have been the wine, the booze.'

'You regret it?'

She noticed his frown. 'No, I didn't mean that. I don't know... but we're both married to other people and... how would it work?'

'I'm serious, I'm divorcing Abi. If it'll make it easier we can leave this place. Together. We'll move out of town.'

'What about Robbie?' Roisin felt torn. She desperately wanted to be swept away by this man; the idea of leaving everything behind and starting again was so appealing. He offered something that was lacking in her life, a new-found joy that had awoken a part of her soul. He made her feel younger, vibrant, loved. His presence was refreshing, like a much needed oasis discovered in a desert, or a cool swift breeze on a hot summer day. The spectre of her former life loomed though, too large to ignore. She couldn't leave her son.

'Bring Robbie.'

'I can't do that to George.'

'Lots of people get divorced. He can still visit the boy, have him at weekends—'

'I don't know.'

'Please.' He put his hands on her shoulders. 'Think about it. Think how happy you are with me and how it could be. Why not leave Robbie with George? We'll have kids of our own.'

'Wh-what?'

'I didn't mean never see him again; we can have him at weekends, maybe.'

Her head spun with conflicting desires and impossible choices. She pulled away from Hugh. 'I really have to go.'

'Okay.' He followed her to the front door. 'Can we meet tomorrow?'

'I don't know.' She turned away to avoid losing herself in his gaze again.

She could almost feel Hugh's eyes on her back as she walked away in a daze.

Once inside her own house, she practically collapsed in a heap behind the door, no longer able to bear the weight of her conscience. 'What have I done?' she said aloud. Tears began to fall.

Chapter Nine

George followed Glen up the stairs.

Glen crouched down when he got to the top. 'He's over there,' he whispered in his friend's ear. 'Stay down.'

'What's he doing?'

'This is too weird; he looks like he's praying to a giant spider on the wall.'

'A s-spider?'

'Not a real one; a great big plastic one. It's on the web he was talking about. It's like a spinning wheel, but it's in the shape of a spider's web. It's got these cocoon-shaped bits: one, two... eight of them.'

'That's what he's planning to put us in?'

'Probably.'

'I say we go and knock him out now. Creep up behind him.'

Glen wiped the sweat from his brow. 'Okay mate, it's all or nothing,' he said, glancing at George distractedly. 'Follow me; we'll knock him out: one of these bricks should do it.' He held up his arm with the chain dangling, brick attached.

George gulped and, with no choice in the matter, followed Glen up the rest of the stairs.

It all happened quickly. Glen ran forward, George tripped up and fell, and the brick attached to the chain on his arm struck the spider-man's legs. *The Spider* grabbed his shin and cried out in agony.

Glen brought his arm up and swung the brick that was attached to the chain so that it made contact with their captor's head.

There was a cracking sound, a lot of blood, more screaming; finally *The Spider* fell backwards onto the wooden web. His weight set off some kind of mechanical device and the web began to rotate on an axle, spinning around and around. The large plastic spider sat in the middle of the wooden contraption, unmoving.

'I-I think he's dead,' said Glen.

George, who had been staring at the wooden web in awe, glanced at Glen then lowered his eyes to see the strange man dressed as a spider now lying on the floor, his head a bloody mess.

'Wh-what do we do now?' stuttered George.

Glen held his forehead for a moment. 'I think we'd better check on the people downstairs, make sure they're all right. Then we'll call the police.'

'He must have the keys for the handcuffs. Check,' said George.

Glen knelt down and contemplated the prone figure on the floor. Wrinkling his nose, he asked, 'Where do you think he keeps them? The spider outfit doesn't look like it's got pockets.'

'He might have clothes underneath.'

'Hang on, yeah, there's a zip.' Glen put his hand on *The Spider*'s chest and pulled the zip to reveal a shirt under the costume; there was a holster attached. 'He's got a gun!' said Glen, taking the weapon out of its holster and handing it to his friend.

George winced. 'Strange gun. It looks more like a water pistol, or something.'

'Take it,' urged Glen. 'And here's some keys, I think.' He rummaged around under the spider costume and eventually drew out a bunch of small keys. 'C'mon,' he said, leaping up. 'Let's go and free the others.'

Glen ran too fast, and George tripped and fell. 'Stop doing that!' George moaned, standing up and holding his knee that was now throbbing.

'Sorry.' Glen moved towards him and tried various keys in the handcuffs. Eventually, one of them worked.

George rubbed his wrists where the cuffs had chafed them.

The two friends went downstairs to the basement.

'Don't you think we should call the police first?' said George.

'Yeah, maybe we should.' Glen reached into his jacket pocket. 'Shit. I don't have my mobile, d'you think that spider-man took it?'

'Dunno, might have fallen from your pocket?' George reached inside his own pocket. 'I've got mine.'

'Great.'

'There's no reception. I'll have to go back upstairs.' George began to ascend the flight of stairs.

The sound of the wooden web spinning around echoed like a threat.

'How do we stop that web from spinning?' Glen wondered aloud.

'Not sure; there must be a button. We'll look for it.'

At the top of the stairs, George stood frozen and Glen bumped into him. 'What are you—'

Both men stared ahead wide-eyed. *The Spider* was getting closer, his gait like that of a zombie.

'D-d-d'you think he's come back from the dead?' whispered Glen.

Limping, blood seeping onto his face, anger in his eyes, the man said, 'You will not get away. You are mere flies. I am The Spider. You will be mine. The web is ready for you.' His words were spoken as if scripted, in a deep and monotonous tone. He stumbled forward.

Both men took a step backwards and fell, losing their footing on the stairs. George landed on Glen's leg as they reached the bottom of the staircase.

'Ow! Quick! The gun, George. Shoot him, now!'

The large shape of their captor loomed at the top of the stairs. 'You'll never win!' he boomed. 'My venom is too powerful.' A spray squirted out from one of the legs in *The Spider*'s costume.

Glen jumped sideways to avoid it, and George put a hand in front of his face. The *venom* hit George's hand.

He screamed. 'My hand! My hand!'

Braying laughter came from the top of the stairs. 'You thought you could win! You cannot beat The Spider!'

'Quick give me the gun!' Glen grabbed the gun from George, who managed to get it from his pocket with his left hand, his right hand painful and burning after being sprayed with the corrosive substance.

Glen hobbled up the stairs, his leg still in pain from when George had fallen on it. He pointed the gun but *The Spider* threw something over him: a kind of netting that he'd pulled out from under his costume. This disoriented Glen, causing him to lose his grip on the gun's trigger. A spindly hand reached out and took the weapon from him while he was trying to figure out a way to free himself from the netting.

George woke up dazed. The pain in his hand was worse, as though he'd plunged it into a pan of boiling oil. On opening his eyes, a dizziness assailed him. It took a moment for him to work out what was happening; his head was near the floor one minute, then near the ceiling the next. His stomach churned with the erratic movement. Astounded, he realised that somehow *The Spider* had managed to secure him to the wooden web. Encasing him was one of the cocoon-shaped structures, which on closer inspection appeared to be lined with a woven fabric. He remembered their captor saying he'd used silk from real spiders; the idea of it made him want to vomit.

He blinked in an attempt to rid his head of the pain, tried to shift his focus to something else. Looking to his right, Glen came into view, also trussed up inside one of the cocoons. The room became hazy as George felt increasingly nauseated from rotating on the wooden web. He had to close his eyes.

'Glen? Glen? Can you hear me?'

George began to cry, acknowledging the futility of the situation. He thought of Robbie and Roisin. Roisin would be cursing him for staying out late. Perhaps she would call the police, or ask Tom and Jess where he'd gone. They'd remember the conversation about the house. He had to hold on to the belief that the police would find them and save them.

Then his mind took a darker turn: what if Roisin spoke to Tom and Jess and they told her about the house, but she didn't call the police, came here herself to find him? She'd be risking her life. His tears continued to fall.

Glen coughed. 'G-George? Wh-what happened? Where are we?'

'You bastard, Glen, we're going to die and it's all your fault.'

'How did we get here?'

'You brought us here, Einstein.'

'No, I was talking about this; this weird web thing.'

'I don't know, just get us off it.'

'Me?'

'It's your fault.'

'Stop whinging; how was I supposed to know? I can't see him anywhere, can you?'

'No,' said George.

'Look, there was a button somewhere: we should try

and hit it to stop the machine, then we can get off.'

'He'll be back soon,' said George through sniffles. 'He's most likely gone to get the other victims.'

'Stop it! We're not victims. Stop thinking like that. We can get away.'

'How? I can't move. I think he must have knocked us out somehow. Drugs maybe? I feel woozy.'

'It's all the spinning, mate. I feel like I'm gonna puke. How do we make it stop?'

'I can't move. I can't do anything.' George's voice sounded high-pitched and it came out as more of a squeal.

'I can move a bit,' said Glen. 'I've got some feeling in my arms.'

'The button was at the bottom; when he tripped on it, he set it off, remember?'

'Right, let me know when we're near the bottom.'

'I can't. Every time I try to open my eyes I feel like I'm gonna be sick.'

'Wait... I think this is the bottom; yes, here, there's a lever. Shit, I missed it. I know where it is though, when I get round there again.'

'Hurry,' said George.

Glen somehow managed to free one arm from the cocoon and reached out as he neared the lever.

Suddenly, and without warning, the machine came to an abrupt halt, causing George to fall out of the cocoon upside down. He slid sideways as he reached towards the floor; landing on his injured hand, he let out a terrifying scream.

'Bloody hell! What happened?' called out Glen from inside his cocoon, struggling to get out. 'Help me, George, don't just sit there!'

'You're the one who pulled the lever, you idiot. You could have warned me.'

'I didn't. It stopped by itself before I pulled the lever.'

'My hand looks like it's been burned. The skin has almost peeled away completely. That must've been acid he sprayed earlier.'

'He's a fucking psycho!'

'Where is he?' asked George, scanning the room.

'God knows. Hey, are you gonna help me out here?' Glen was half hanging off the contraption.

'Yeah, er... sorry.' George helped Glen to escape the cocoon.

After falling onto the floor, Glen picked himself up and wiped some of the dust from his trousers. 'The web must've broken; it just stopped, just like that.'

'Hopefully that means Mr Spider won't be able to use it.'

Glen scanned the room, then, in hushed tones, said, 'It's pretty weird how that freak survived his head being smashed in. D'you think the spider bite might have given him some kind of special power?'

'You've been watching too many sci-fi movies.'

'Let's hope that's what it is.' Glen frowned. 'He must have some strength if he managed to put us in the cocoon.'

'D'you think there's somebody helping him?'

'They say mad men have the strength of ten. Let's go and get the others and get out of here.'

'No, we should just go,' said George, pulling Glen's arm to stop him. 'I think he must be down there. We can't risk seeing him again.'

'You're right.'

'Not so fast,' boomed a familiar voice behind them as they headed for the door.

The Spider stood at the top of the stairs that led down to the basement, holding a gun, pointing it at them. Half of his face was covered in blood. He swayed from side to side.

Glen fell to the floor.

'Gl-Glen!' George stuttered as panic set in.

Glen lay prone, face down.

'It appears that your friend isn't as brave as he makes himself out to be,' said *The Spider*, his speech slurred and slower than usual.

George looked at him and then back at Glen, noticing his friend's hand reaching for one of the bricks that they'd freed themselves from earlier.

'W-we have to get help for my friend,' he said to *The Spider*, hoping to distract him so he didn't work out what Glen was up to.

The man glared at George and then began to laugh.

Glen grabbed the brick, jumped up, and ran towards *The Spider*, smashing the brick against the man's head a couple of times.

The Spider dropped his gun and slid backwards, tumbling down the stairs to the basement.

'He's got to be dead now, surely!' said Glen.

George put his hand to his mouth.

Glen ran over to him, 'Let's get outta here.'

George's phone sounded. It was on the floor, under the wooden web. He bent down and picked it up. 'Hello.'

'Hi,' said Roisin. 'Where are you?'

'Wh-what time is it?'

'Eleven-thirty.'

'Sorry. I lost track of time, that's all. I'll be home soon.'

'Okay, don't be too long.'

'I'll see you later.'

Glen peered at him. 'Roisin?'

'Yeah. It's only eleven-thirty. For some reason I thought we'd been here over night.'

'That's 'cos we've been knocked out so many times. Why didn't you tell her about the house?'

'No, I don't want her involved.'

'Fine, call the cops and we'll get out of here.'

'Right.' George dialled 999.

'Eight Goldfern Road?' said the policeman.

'Yes,' said George.

'How did you get in?'

'Through the door.'

'Yes, but was it locked?'

'Um... My friend opened it. I think it was unlocked.' He shrugged and looked at Glen, who shrugged back at him.

'Are there any other people at the house?' asked the policeman.

'I-I think so; the man said there were other hostages, eight... no, six other hostages. Eight including us.'

'Are they alive?'

'I think so. Will you be sending someone?'

'What made you enter the house?'

'Er... we were just curious; it was vacant for so long...'

'Where is the man who threatened to kill you?'

'He's here... He's dead, we think. We were trying to escape. My friend hit him with a brick. We were defending ourselves... He was planning to kill us.'

'We'll be sending some officers over to take statements from you and the other hostages. Please go to the front of the house and meet us there.'

George ended the call: 'We have to meet the police at the front of the house.'

'But what about the sleeping-spider gas? What if we accidentally activate it again?'

'Let's climb out of the window.'

'But they're boarded up!'

69

'Get one of the bricks, we can use it to knock the boards out.'

A police car was pulling up in front of the house as they exited.

George nudged Glen and pointed to the house next door. Theo was standing at his door wearing a dressing gown.

'What's going on boys? Were you in the house? I head some noise,' shouted the old man.

'It's all right, Theo. You can go back to bed. Everything's fine here,' said Glen.

Theo walked towards them.

'What happened in there?' he asked, frowning.

'Rex was in there. He's been keeping hostages. He wanted to kill us,' said George.

'Oh my God. Are you all right? Why did you go in there?'

'We're fine; at least the police are here now,' said Glen.

Two police officers approached.

'You should go back home,' said Glen to Theo.

Theo nodded and walked back to his house.

Glen and George spent the next few hours giving statements to the police, along with the rest of the hostages. It appeared that all the hostages had been well fed and cared for by *The Spider.*

Chapter Ten

Roisin sat at the kitchen table staring at the clock. 12.30 a.m.

Inside, she was fuming. George had said he'd be home "soon" at 11.30 p.m. *Where is he?*

She imagined he was still at the pub with Glen and maybe Tom and Jess. They'd all gone to university together and had so many in-jokes that she often felt uncomfortable going out with them. George usually invited her, but she mostly declined.

He'd hardly ever been out with her group of friends, either. The more she thought about it, the more she realised how different they were.

Staring at her mobile on the table in front of her, she debated whether she should call George again. *Why should I? He should be calling me, explaining why he's late.* Despite the irritation, a worry crept into her mind because he'd never before stayed out this late without letting her know where he was.

Tonight her impatience to see him was twofold, not only to make sure he was all right, but because she'd convinced herself that when she saw him again everything would make sense: when George came home, she'd know for certain that her fling with Hugh had been merely a kind of revolt against the stagnation of her life—a momentary lapse of reason. As soon as he returned home, the equilibrium would be restored. The longer he remained out, the more her thoughts were turning to Hugh.

Surprising herself, Roisin went to her bedroom and began to get changed. It was a decision made in some part of her brain that had resolved that action was needed. A desire to be with Hugh was taking over. She didn't try to question what she was doing, or why, or whether it was right or wrong.

Usually at this time of night she'd change into her pyjamas, but tonight she pulled on her favourite dress. She'd last worn it more than a year ago, to the office Christmas party. It was a slinky black dress.

As she caught sight of her reflection in the mirror, she tried to imagine what Hugh's reaction would be when he saw her. A guilty feeling descended when she remembered how George had complimented her when she'd first worn it.

'Wow, Roisin! You look gorgeous in that dress.'
'Thanks. Don't I always look gorgeous?'
'Of course. In fact, it's only gorgeous because you're wearing it.'

She recalled how he'd kissed her and the memory merged with the way Hugh had kissed her. Sitting on the bed, opposite the mirror, she looked at her wedding ring and closed her eyes.

Wearing the dress reminded her how happy she'd once been with George. Many of her colleagues at the office party had said they looked great together; he'd been so attentive. They were described as "the perfect couple".

Roisin wondered whether those times were lost in the past now; could her relationship with George ever go back to what it once was? She touched the silky material on the skirt of the dress.

After questioning for the tenth time what she was about to do, she picked up her handbag from the bed where she'd discarded it earlier when returning from next door. She slipped on her four-inch black heels and walked out of the bedroom.

Stopping outside Robbie's room, she popped her head around the door: *I'll only be next door,* she thought. Feeling dreadful and fighting with her conscience, she ran into the bathroom and rummaged around in the bottom draw of the cabinet. *Where is it?* She breathed a sigh of relief as the baby-monitor came into view.

She went into the boy's room, plugged in the transmitter and put the receiver in her bag, switching it on as she left the house.

As she stood waiting outside Hugh and Abigail's front door, Roisin worried that George might walk up the path to their house at any moment and see her.

Hugh opened the door wearing a pair of jeans, nothing else. She stared at his bare chest and a flood of colour rushed to her cheeks as she remembered the passion they'd shared; she wanted him to wrap his arms around her again. A tear came to her eye, confusion over what she was doing.

'Couldn't keep away, hey?' he said, an eyebrow raised. 'You look stunning. That's a very sexy dress.'

Suddenly self-conscious, she spluttered, 'C-can... er... I um... come in?'

'Of course.' He opened the door wider and waved her inside with a flourish of his hand. 'Nice perfume,' he said, leaning towards her.

She felt embarrassed that she'd dressed up for him and sprayed herself liberally with her favourite perfume—the one George said he couldn't resist. She thought of little Robbie and turned around again when she reached the living room doorway, intending to leave.

Hugh placed his hands on her shoulders. 'Something's wrong,' he said. 'Have you been crying?'

A tear fell from her eye as she looked up at him. 'I'm so sorry; I'm such a mess. I shouldn't be here.'

'Well, you're here now. I'll get you a drink.' Taking her hand, he led her into the living room, then made his way to the bar.

She sat on the sofa in a virtual replay of that evening.

After placing her handbag on the floor, she covered her face with her hands.

'Roisin?'

She peeked out from between her hands, then reached out for the glass of wine he was holding towards her, and downed it.

He sat next to her. 'What's happened?'

'I shouldn't be here. My son is asleep next door. I should be there, but I wanted to be here. I don't want to be there. It's George.'

'Wh-what happened? Did he find out about us?'

'No. He's always with his friends, in the pub. He's not back yet. I phoned him at half-eleven and he said he'd be home soon.'

'I'm sorry,' said Hugh.

'What happened before... that was just me wanting some attention. You were so... I mean, you're the first man who's shown me that kind of affection in ages. It's so... Me and George have become like the typical married couple who live separate lives. We don't have anything in common anymore. I find myself snapping at him. I'm sorry to have got you involved in this. I shouldn't have slept with you today.'

'I've told you how I feel, Roisin. I'm divorcing Abi. You can move in with me.' He took her hands. 'This seems to be perfect timing. Both of us are unhappy in our marriages. We should be together.'

For a moment, she was lost again in the melody of his voice and the sparkle of his eyes.

'Daddy,' the muffled voice came followed by a few sniffles and then repeated, 'Daddy.'

'The baby monitor,' she said, reaching for her handbag. 'Robbie's woken up. I've got to go. Sorry, Hugh. We'll talk about this.'

Hugh stood up and held her close to him. 'Please, come over tomorrow.'

'I'm working, and then I have to pick up Robbie from school.'

'In the evening. Tell George you're meeting friends. He can't exactly object after what he's done today, can he?'

She heard more sniffling through the baby monitor. 'Sorry, Hugh. I'll try to get away tomorrow evening.'

He kissed her and she found herself kissing him back, wishing she could stay.

He pulled away when Robbie's voice sounded over the monitor: 'Daddy!'

Roisin ran to the front door, narrowly avoiding tripping in her heels.

'See you tomorrow,' he said as he watched her leave.

Chapter Eleven

Rex survived, despite the blows he'd received to his head. He was admitted to hospital and a psychiatric ward for a few weeks. Eventually, he was allowed back to his home at 8 Goldfern Road.

Theo invited George and Glen to his house for his 80th Birthday celebration. That's when they found out Rex had moved back next door.

'Oh my God, The Spider?' George blurted.

'He's a nice man. In fact, he'll be coming to my party a little later,' said Theo. 'He had a breakdown, that's why he did the spider thing. He's totally embarrassed by it now, so we don't mention it. I thought it would be nice for you two to meet him now and see how he's changed. After what he put you through. I warned you about the house. I still can't understand why you went in there.'

'It was curiosity,' said George.

Theo shrugged. 'Anyway, you might be able to see Dave tonight.'

'Who's Dave?' asked Glen.

'The man you used to know, who lived next door before Rex. It's one of the reasons I asked you here tonight.'

'Oh, *Dave*. Yes.'

'I found his number a couple of weeks ago and invited him. I mentioned you but he couldn't remember you. He said he would try to come, but he's having family problems so might not be able to make it. If he doesn't, remind me to give you his number before you leave, okay?'

'Er... yeah, okay. Thanks,' said Glen.

'If nothing else, it will be good for you to see Rex now.'

'I'm surprised he's out of prison so quickly,' said George, grumpily, 'after what he did.'

'I don't know the ins-and-outs, but I think he paid a top lawyer, and because it was mental illness they were lenient.'

'Huh, the rich always get away with their crimes,' snorted Glen.

'I think you'll change your mind when you meet him again,' said Theo. 'I know you boys had a terrible time in there, but Rex wasn't himself. The police understood that, which is why they reduced the punishment. It's some kind of suspended sentence, I think, and he has to comply with their rules. He told me all about it. Rex often comes round for tea. You'll never believe that he's now friends with most of his hostages. After he found out what he'd done, he contacted them and offered to make up for it. As Rex is quite wealthy, he helped the homeless man and squatters to get back on their feet, helped them find somewhere to live. So, you see, he's not such a monster.'

'Wow,' said Glen and George together.

'I don't know if I want to see that weirdo again,' said George when Theo had gone to mingle with the other party guests.

'You heard what Theo said, he's better now. It was a breakdown, or something.'

'Yeah, but what if he flips again?'

Glen laughed. 'Why would he?'

'I dunno, what if he sees us and it makes him remember everything.'

'You worry too much, George. Look on the bright side; apparently the man's minted. He might wanna make it up to us and give us some money.'

'Is money all you think about?'

'Pretty much. I'm getting another beer, want one?'

'Yeah, thanks.' George fixed his eyes on the front door

as his friend went to get their drinks. He'd been having nightmares ever since being captured by *The Spider*, and was growing increasingly nervous of falling asleep at night; it had almost become a phobia. He hadn't told anyone.

'Boo!' said Glen, returning with the drinks.

George jumped.

'Blimey, you're very highly strung today.' Glen handed him a can of beer.

'Thanks,' he mumbled.

'Hi,' said a young woman who looked familiar. 'I'm Lisa, from number six. You're the guys who came to ask about the house next door, aren't you? I heard about what happened. You were so brave.' She fluttered her eyelashes at Glen.

George couldn't help but notice. 'It was all Glen's work. He's the real hero; saved us both.'

Lisa grinned.

Glen gawped at George, who winked back at him.

'I hear Rex has been invited here today,' said George.

Lisa leaned in and whispered to them both: 'To be honest, he still freaks me out. If I tell you something, do you promise not to tell anyone?'

'Yeah,' said Glen and George together.

'A couple of nights ago, he was in his back garden wearing a spider costume. He's only done it once, as far as I know, but I'm worried he's going crazy again.'

'Maybe you should tell someone,' said George.

'Yeah,' said Glen. 'He might need help.'

'I told Theo and he said that he saw him too but he doesn't think it's a problem.'

'Sounds a bit weird to me,' said Glen.

'Yes, it is. He sang that song, "Itsy Bitsy Spider".'

'"Incy Wincy Spider"?' said George.

'Yeah, that's the one. He sang it really slowly in a deep

78

voice. It woke me up; it must've been about two o'clock in the morning. Really creepy.'

'I thought you were gonna move away from here,' said Glen.

'I was, but when you two rescued the hostages I thought that was the end of the problem. I do like this area.'

'Yes, it's a nice area, I s'pose. Me and George wanted to buy the house next door, do it up, sell it on. You can get a good price for properties round here. That's why we went into the house in the first place, to check it out.'

'Maybe you should ask Spiderman if he's interested in selling. I'd much rather have you as a neighbour,' said Lisa. She smiled brightly at Glen. 'A *real* superhero.'

The doorbell rang.

'I'll get that!' shouted Theo over the loud music.

Moments later, George and Glen were standing face to face with their former captor.

The colour drained from George's face. A dizzy feeling came over him and he prayed he wouldn't faint.

'H-hello, Rex,' said Glen.

The man who had been so confident and loud as *The Spider* only a few months before, now appeared subdued. He had his head down and lifted his eyes towards Glen. 'Um, I just want to say I'm sorry for everything.'

'No need to apologise. We heard about what happened,' said Glen.

Rex's eyes glistened and he nodded.

George remained silent, wishing the man would go away. He still felt fearful of him, even though he looked so small now without his spider costume and so ordinary without his make-up. There was something eerie about the way he stared straight ahead at them, looking from him to Glen without any real emotion in his eyes: eyes that were the darkest shade of brown. George wondered whether it was a trick of the light that they shone black, almost as if the pupil had grown to completely cover the iris.

Rex shuffled away following Theo, much to George's relief.

'That was weird. He's nothing like his alter ego.' Glen chuckled.

George didn't respond.

'You all right, George?'

'Yeah, fine. I think I need a whisky.'

'So, are you gonna ask him if you can buy his house?' asked Lisa, fluttering her eyelashes at Glen again.

'Um... Not sure. Don't think I can afford it, to be honest.'

'After everything that happened, you should ask him if you can buy it cheap. He's loaded, apparently.'

'Dunno, wouldn't that be kinda wrong? The man was mentally ill when it happened.'

'Yeah, but you could be scarred for life. He owes you,' said Lisa.

George walked away, heading for the kitchen.

Glen followed him.

When they were in the kitchen and Lisa was out of earshot, George said, 'Why did you give Lisa such a hard time about her suggestion? You practically said the same thing earlier.'

'What did I say?' Glen sneered.

'You said we might be able to get some money from him because of what he did to us.'

'Yeah, I know, but I was just saying it—and... it's none of her business.'

'Do you fancy her?'

'Are you off your rocker or something? She's so

80

annoying.'

'She fancies you. It's obvious. And you'd make a good team, always searching for the next get-rich-quick scheme.'

'Give it a rest. I'm not interested in her.'

George poured a whisky for himself. 'Want one?'

'No, I'm sticking to beer, thanks.' Glen grabbed a can of beer. 'Y'know, if it's true that this man has a lot of money, it wouldn't hurt to try and get the house next door at a knock-down price. He did freaking keep us hostage and was planning to kill us. You've been acting strange since then.'

'What do you mean "strange"?' George peered at him.

'Y'know, highly strung, jittery.'

'Jittery? I'm not fucking jittery.'

'Look, no offence, mate, but you have to admit it's made you wary, more scared of your shadow.'

'Fuck off.'

'All I'm saying is, we could sue the man for emotional distress, but we're not, are we? We're only asking for some money off the price of the house.'

'I'd rather not kick a man when he's down; it wasn't his fault he had a breakdown. You go ahead, Glen.'

'Your loss. I'll be sitting on that beach on my own next year, then.'

'Why don't you take Lisa with you?' huffed George as he returned to the living room.

Towards the end of the evening, most people had left the party. Theo was saying goodbye to his youngest daughter at the front door.

Glen and George were sitting on the sofa. George had been drinking all evening and was now the worse for wear.

'I'm gonna talk to him about buying that house,' said

Glen.

'Uh?' George looked at him bleary-eyed.

'You drunk?'

'No.'

'What's up with you? You haven't been the same since —,'

'Since what? Since—'

'Since the... y'know the spider-man incident. You've changed.'

George seemed to suddenly wake up and straightened his posture. 'Of course I'm not the same! That man nearly killed us... and he would, you know... he would'a done.'

'He didn't though. You've got to try and get over it.'

Blinking a few times, George slurred, 'H-how can you be sho...'

Glen shrugged. 'It's over. It's in the past.'

George sighed and leaned back on the sofa. 'It's not only that. There's something else.' He stared into his empty beer can.

'What?'

'I think Roisin's having an affair.'

'I thought you two were happy.'

'We were... We are... I dunno; it's the way she ogles the man next door as if he's some kind of hunk. A few weeks back we were at the parents' evening at Robbie's school, and when we bumped into him Roisin started fluttering her eyelashes.'

'But... he's married, right?'

'Yeah, but his wife's left him, and he seems to get on well with Roisin. They ended up chatting together while I was stuck talking to one of the teachers, and the way she was looking at him... I suppose I've only got myself to blame; the way I've been since Rex got us. Me and Roisin haven't slept together since. It's like I'm cursed.'

'You've got to snap out of it. I think you're being paranoid about your neighbour. Maybe she fancies him, but *Roisin*? I don't think she'd have an affair. She's too straight-laced.'

'Yeah, but I've been neglecting her.'

'So don't. Um... I don't wanna be insensitive or anything, but we have more important stuff to think about.'

'Huh?' George had reverted to his half-asleep state.

'The house next door,' said Glen. 'Lisa's right; he's scarred us for life and we should try to get compensation for that. He's ruined our lives: even your marriage could be down the drain because of it.'

'D'you fancy Lisa?' asked George.

'No, you plonker; she's too thin, I've told you that.'

'She's put on a bit of weight since we last saw her.'

'She'll probably end up fat then. I'm not interested. All I'm saying is, she had a point about the house.'

'Whatever. I still think you fancy her.'

'Think what you like.'

Lisa was sitting on the other side of the room talking to one of Theo's daughters; every now and then she'd peer across at Glen as if hoping to catch his eye.

'You could do a lot worse,' said George. 'She keeps looking over at you. She definitely fancies you. You should go for it. What have you got to lose?'

'My sanity,' said Glen. 'Anyway, who are you to give relationship advice when your marriage is down the toilet?'

'Oi.'

'Sorry, no offence. Listen, I'm gonna ask Mr Spider if he'll sell us his house at a bargain price.'

'Count me out.'

'C'mon. I won't be able to afford it without you, and you get half the profits when it sells.'

'I'd have to speak to Roisin.'

'No, don't get her involved.'

'She's my wife.'

'Yeah, for how much longer? In this life you've got to take care of yourself.'

'She'd definitely leave me if I did something like that behind her back.'

'Not if you made a nice tidy profit and treated her to a nice holiday.'

'Hmm...'

'So, what d'ya say?'

'Maybe.'

Rex was sitting on an armchair next to Theo, Theo's eldest daughter, and Lisa—the only other people in the room. Theo's middle daughter and her two children were cleaning in the kitchen.

Rex watched as Glen walked towards him.

'Eight,' said Rex.

'Um... sorry?'

'There are eight of you left. The perfect number.'

Glen averted his eyes from the man's hard stare. Recollections of the time locked in the dark room in the basement of the house next door flooded his mind and filled him with a sense of unease. He took a couple of steps back, then sat on a chair next to the man. Taking a deep breath, he said, 'Listen mate, I want to let bygones be bygones, forgive and forget and all that.'

Rex was staring straight ahead.

'Um, excuse me, Rex.'

'Yes, yes, I heard you.'

'Great, well, um... You must want to put it all behind you and start afresh. It must be hard living next door. Me and my friend George over there would be interested in buying your house.'

'You want my house?' Rex looked at him, and for a moment Glen could have sworn the man's eyes were completely black with no iris and no pupil. He blinked and was relieved to find he must have imagined it.

Glen caught his breath and said, 'My friend's been suffering with nightmares since what happened, and I've also lost sleep. George might even end up divorced because he hasn't been able to... you know, sleep with his wife because of what you did; he's traumatised.'

Rex turned away. 'I don't see what that has to do with you wanting to buy the house,' he mumbled.

'We're not planning to live there: too many memories, as I said—but we were thinking of buying it and renting it out, or selling it. After everything that's happened, we wanted to know if you'd agree a price with us of let's say, two hundred thousand.'

'You really want to buy the house?'

'Yeah.'

'Two hundred thousand, you say?'

'Yeah.' Glen nodded enthusiastically.

'Why don't I go and tidy up a bit, then you can come and have a look. I've made changes since the last time—'

Glen waved his hand as if to dismiss the idea, 'I'm sure it's fine.'

Rex rose from his seat, 'Come and knock next door. Give me about ten minutes. Bring Theo and the others. We can have a nightcap at mine, for old times' sake.'

'Cool. And you'll consider selling it?' Glen stood up.

'Yes, it seems like a reasonable offer... in the circumstances.' Rex picked up the ladle that had been in the punch bowl and knocked it on the glass coffee table three times. 'Can I have your attention, please?' he shouted loudly. 'Drinks next door, on me, in ten minutes—to celebrate friends and moving on. I'm selling my house to George and

Glen.'

'Sounds great!' said Theo. 'Congratulations, boys,' he said to Glen and George, holding up his wine glass.

'Yay! I'm so excited!' squealed Lisa. She stood up and approached Glen. 'You'll be moving in next door!'

Glen avoided her arms that were extended as if she were waiting for a hug. 'Er... not moving in, exactly, just doing it up and selling it on.'

Lisa's arms fell to her sides and her smile faded slightly. 'B-but you'll be around for a while. Are you doing the renovating yourself?' she asked hopefully.

'No, I've got some builder mates.'

Lisa's face dropped.

'Come in, come in; the door's on the latch.'

The eight of them stood outside 8 Goldfern Road.

'I'm in the kitchen, be out in two secs,' shouted Rex from inside the house.

They entered and stood in the hallway then one by one went down like flies.

Half an hour later, they were rotating on the wheel of the giant wooden spiderweb.

George opened his eyes, and slowly realised what had happened. They'd been trapped, just like the last time. He couldn't understand how they had all been drugged and placed in the silk cocoons on the spiderweb, was unable to fathom how one man had been able to do that.

His question was soon answered as Rex appeared, dressed in his furry costume. On either side of him stood a burly man.

'Meet my friends,' said Rex.

The eight people continued to spin around on the contraption.

'These fine men helped me capture you all. They've been living with me in my basement since they escaped from prison, a couple of weeks ago. They've agreed to help me put my plan into action.' *The Spider* clapped his hands. 'Get the petrol, boys. This place will explode into flames! It will be my pièce de résistance. When I leave here, I will have won. I will be remembered as *The Spider*. I will have won!' He punched the air.

The two heavily built criminals disappeared down the stairs that led to the basement.

Unexpectedly, the machine stopped spinning.

'Wh-what? That can't be happening.' Rex's voice came out sounding high-pitched.

George and Lisa, who were at the bottom of the web, slid out of their cocoons.

Lisa immediately reached to take Glen's hand and helped him get out of the cocoon.

Rex produced a weird-looking gun and pointed it at them.

Glen ran towards him without thinking, and—taking him unawares—grabbed the gun.

'Glen!' George shouted. 'Be careful!'

Glen shot at Rex. The gun sprayed some kind of jet spray of fluid that seemed to knock out *The Spider;* he collapsed onto the floor. 'Quick, we've gotta get out!'

The two criminals were now at the top of the stairs carrying petrol canisters.

Glen shot the fluid at them both and they keeled over.

Glen, George, and Lisa helped the others out of the cocoons and then headed for the living room window, wary of walking through the hallway because of the sleeping-spider gas.

George, the last person to exit the house, hesitated at the window.

'What the hell are you waiting for?' screamed Glen, 'Hurry up!'

'You go on, I won't be long!' George called out.

A few minutes later, George exited the building puffing and panting. 'Get back, get back!' he screamed out.

Everyone ran over to the other side of the road.

A massive explosion caused all eight to be thrown back onto the ground. The house filled with billowing flames, and the windows burst from their frames, spraying fragments of glass all over the road.

'G-George? Did you?' Glen raised his eyebrows.

'I don't know what happened,' he said quickly. 'I only went back in to look for my phone, it'd fallen out when I was in the cocoon. I think them men must've spilt some petrol when they fell over. I have no idea what happened to set the place on fire.' George was staring at the remains of the house as he spoke.

George was questioned by the police about the destruction of the house, as he was the last person to come out alive. He was released without charge as there was no firm evidence to prove how the house had burnt down.

The deaths of Rex and his two criminal cohorts were treated as "death by misadventure" at the inquest.

Chapter Twelve

Roisin stared at her face in the bathroom mirror. She wanted to scream, hardly recognising the person looking back at her. *Who are you? Who? I would never have done that.* She thought of Robbie and an instant panic set in; he could be up to anything, doing something dangerous. The silence frightened her. She'd been in the bathroom—locked herself in—for at least fifteen minutes.

She scrabbled to the bathroom door and fiddled with the lock, grabbed the handle and ran outside. Her face was flushed. 'Robbie!' she shouted. 'Robbie! Where are you?'

No reply. Not unusual for Robbie. When he was younger, she'd lost him in the house a few times and he'd ignore her when she called out his name; her heart would beat in her mouth by the time she found him, often hidden in a cupboard or under a bed. He'd smile as if he'd done nothing wrong and she'd hug him, so relieved to finally find him.

'Where are you?' she screamed at the top of her voice. She stumbled into his room and saw him sitting on his bed playing a game with some plastic action figures.

'What's wrong, Mummy?' he asked, innocently. 'Where's Daddy?'

'He's out,' bitterness seeped into her voice as she said it. 'C'mon, let's get you ready for bed.'

'But, I want Daddy to read me a story.'

'He had to work late. *I'll* read you a story.'

'But you don't do the voices.'

'I'll do the voices.' She frowned, doubting she'd be able to concentrate on a story with her brain working overtime as it was.

Somehow, she managed to put the boy to bed and read

him a story, on automatic pilot. At 9 p.m. she trundled down the stairs and sat in the living room silently cursing George. He'd gone out with Glen again, some mutual friend's birthday party. *He drove me to it*, she muttered silently to herself. *If he'd been around I wouldn't have slept with Hugh.*

It was late, and she was mindful that George could return home at any moment; she'd left the pregnancy tests in the bathroom. Three of them.

When the first one spelt out the word "Pregnant", she'd assumed it must be faulty. The second one confirmed the result, and tears followed. She'd held the third pregnancy test to her chest and prayed, as if holding a religious artefact. *Please, please, I'll do anything, please let the others have been wrong.*

She'd sat in the bathroom on the toilet seat lid in stunned silence for a while after the third test revealed the same result. She thought of the fifteen pounds she'd spent to find out what she already knew.

She was pregnant and not certain who the father was, but suspected it was Hugh. Her guilt about sleeping with the neighbour had made it practically impossible for any kind of closeness with her husband.

It turned out that George had sustained an injury at work, which was why he'd returned home late that first night when she'd gone back to Hugh's house and had assumed George didn't care about her. His hand was in a bandage when he got home in the middle of the night. He'd suffered some kind of acid burn and said he didn't want to worry her, so hadn't called. Her heart jumped when she heard that. To think, that night she'd considered sleeping with Hugh again, had got dressed in her favourite dress and heels, all because she believed George had neglected her, but all the while he was suffering and not wanting her to worry.

She'd felt like a bad person for ages, but Hugh had

enticed her to his house on a number of occasions since then; she'd mostly managed to make excuses, but did succumb to his charms a few more times, usually in a state of drunkenness and without stopping to consider using contraception.

George had been distant and she'd been weak-willed, unable to resist when Hugh offered his affections. Each time she slept with him the burden of guilt became heavier and harder to carry, so eventually she put an end to it, telling Hugh she couldn't see him again. That was a couple of weeks ago.

Abigail had left Hugh for good now. She'd taken Liam and was staying with her parents—that much Roisin knew, but she hadn't stopped to talk with Hugh for long recently, not trusting herself, fearing they'd end up sleeping together again.

In the past couple of weeks, Hugh had started drinking, she'd noticed. A lot. He had stopped shaving, or washing, judging by his outward appearance. His hair was messy, greasy, and he'd lost the sparkle in his green eyes; his stained clothes looked like they needed to be ironed.

Whenever he spoke to her lately, his speech was slurred. She'd often wondered whether he was an alcoholic while they were having their affair because of the amount of whisky he consumed.

She went to the bathroom and retrieved the three pregnancy tests. After running downstairs as if her life depended on it, she opened the front door and dumped the evidence in the bin. *What am I going to do now?* she asked herself, as she traipsed into the living room.

Chapter Thirteen

Rex had bequeathed the proceeds of sale of 8 Goldfern Road to Glen and George in his will. The will had been drawn up a few days after he'd been released from hospital, so it was assumed he was compos mentis at the time. There were no close relatives who might want to contest his will, in any event. George and Glen discovered that Rex had been an only child; both his parents were killed in a house fire when he was seventeen years old and since then he'd lived alone. He'd taken over the successful family business—a jeweller's shop owned by his late father—and sold it five years before the tragic events at Goldfern Road, for over three million pounds. That went some way to explaining how he'd accumulated so much wealth.

With mixed feelings, Glen and George took the keys of the property from Rex's solicitor when the reading of the will was over. The house had been completely gutted by the fire. According to the insurance company's findings, there were signs that the place had been doused with petrol, set alight on purpose. In the circumstances, the building insurance policy didn't cover the damage. They came to an agreement with the executors of the estate that Glen could instruct his builder friends to repair the damage to enable a sale of the property to go ahead. As the proceeds were to go to George and Glen, they were the people with the most interest in any money being made from a sale; it was also decided that it would be wrong for the executors to use money from the estate to repair the house because no stipulation about that had been made in the will.

Glen and George stood outside the burnt-out shell that used to be 8 Goldfern Road.

Glen turned to his friend, narrowing his eyes; 'George, I'm only gonna ask you once, mate, but I want you to tell me the truth, okay?'

George shrugged. 'About what?'

'Did you set this place on fire?'

George's eyes sprang open and he shot Glen a look. 'No!'

'Okay, okay; I only asked.'

'D'you really think I'd risk my life in there when I have a kid?' His mind went back to when he'd been in the house that night; he couldn't remember what made him do it, only that he wanted to make sure Rex didn't get out alive. He'd rushed in and grabbed a petrol canister that was lying on the floor beside one of the criminals. The large man started to stir and George was worried he might grab his leg, or somehow manage to stop him leaving the house. He'd poured petrol all over the man's face and watched as some of it spilled into his mouth. The man's eyes had bulged then and he'd begun spitting out the petrol and coughing. At that point, the other criminal began to move.

George had grabbed the other canister and started pouring petrol everywhere trying to avoid splashing himself.

Once outside the living room window, he lit a match and threw it into the room before darting across the road.

Something told him that if Rex was dead he'd stop having the nightmares, would be free. But the bad dreams raged on and they became progressively worse, and were now fuelled by his guilt over the murders. He'd extinguished three people's lives and he'd done it on purpose.

'Sorry, mate. But I needed to know, y'know?' Glen's voice disturbed his reverie.

'It's a ruin,' mumbled George. 'We should put it down to *The Spider* having a last laugh at our expense. What can we do with this dump?'

'It's fine. My builder mates will do the place up for us and we can pay them when we sell it.'

'But why did he leave the place to us? It doesn't make sense.'

'You're probably right that it was a last laugh at our expense. After all, he didn't leave us the house, did he? He left us the "proceeds of sale". He was probably planning to burn it down before he died.'

'Hmm. It still doesn't really make sense.'

'I can't get my head round it, either,' said Glen. 'Let's just imagine that he felt guilty about what happened, how much he'd scared us.'

'If that had been the reason, he would have included the others in the will too. They'd been locked up, trapped here for so long.'

'Maybe he fancied you.' Glen giggled.

'Idiot,' said George, shivering as an image of his last sight of the man flashed before him: lying on the floor, the sprawling ridiculous furry spider suit all around him. George had noticed his eyes as he rushed out of the room. He'd spent countless sleepless nights wondering about the look in those eyes. What were his last thoughts? No conclusion had ever been reached in George's mind, but the memory remained.

'Remember what Theo said at the party,' said Glen. 'Rex helped out the others when he got out of hospital, right? It was only us left to help. I suppose that's why he decided to leave the house to us in his will.'

'Still doesn't add up, because if he was planning to kill us anyway, why would he do that?'

'I actually don't think he was planning to kill us when he wrote the will. He must've had another mental breakdown, or something, afterwards.'

'He was creepy.'

'Yeah, well, he's gone now. And this is our legacy. Looks like my dream of escaping from the rat race might not be so unrealistic.' Glen held up the keys as they stood at the front door. He laughed. 'Why did they give us the keys? The door exploded in the fire.'

George let out a dry laugh. Taking a deep breath, he followed his friend into the remains of *The Spider*'s lair.

Chapter Fourteen

In the middle of the night, George was shaken from his sleep by words that came from out of nowhere, '*It has become my mission to destroy you!*' The words boomed, yet he seemed to be the only one who'd heard them; Roisin was fast asleep next to him. Flashes of light entered through the bedroom window and he caught sight of her profile each time the lightning struck. Heavy rain pelted against the window as if it were trying to find a way in.

On hearing a loud crack of thunder, George felt as frightened as a child alone in a dark bedroom and wanted to wake Roisin. He'd been sweating while asleep, as if he had a fever; the back of his neck was wet.

Another lightning strike flashed. He noticed a figure silhouetted against the window. *Rex?* The shape of the furry, spider costume was unmistakable. But how could that be? Rex was dead. George blinked and the figure disappeared.

Taking a deep breath, George stepped out of his bed and wiped the perspiration from his brow. He made his way downstairs to the kitchen for a glass of water, all the time feeling as though someone, or some*thing*, was following him, but there was no one there.

When he switched on the light his fear dissipated, but then the tablecloth began to rise from the kitchen table and flapped about before him. A deep, harsh laugh reverberated around the room, a laugh he recognised but couldn't place. George stood still, unable to move.

'*I am The Spider.*' The words resounded and echoed in the room, but George knew that they were only in his head. They had to be only in his head. The words replayed and at the same time scribbles appeared on one of the walls: a script written by a shaky hand, spelt out, "I am The Spider. I will win."

The writing disappeared after another lightning strike. *It's late, I'm tired; traumatised. It's a nightmare. It's because we went to the house today, that's all.* He traipsed over to the sink and poured himself a glass of water.

As he reached to place the empty glass in the sink, a spider crawled up towards his hand, causing him to flinch and almost drop the glass. The spider stopped moving. Although merely a centimetre in diameter, it frightened him more than any spider he'd ever seen. It was dark and furry, reminding him of the costume worn by Rex. The creature crawled along the bottom of the sink.

George turned on the hot tap, twisting it as far as it would go until it splashed water all around the sides of the sink and even onto the shirt of his pyjamas. He jumped back when the heat of the water burned him through the thin shirt. On lifting his pyjama top he saw a red mark on his tummy that made him think of the burns sustained on his hand at 8 Goldfern Road, and the lie he'd told Roisin to cover up the truth. He still hadn't breathed a word to her about Rex or the house. It made him question his reasons. After all, it wasn't a secret. The police knew about it. It had even been in the local newspaper—although, thankfully, his and Glen's names weren't mentioned. Roisin didn't read the papers, anyway; she didn't watch the news as she thought it was too depressing.

They hardly spoke to each other anymore. Were they just hanging on to a hopeless relationship?

His thoughts had distracted him so that when he finally tuned back into what was happening in the kitchen, the sink was nearly half full of steaming water. George watched as the spider floated up in the waves. He switched off the tap, and the arachnid eventually disappeared down the drain in a spiral of water.

He backed away and made to leave the kitchen. The tablecloth lay on the table undisturbed and there was nothing written on the wall; everything was as it should be. He cursed his mind, even managed a smile at his nonsensical thoughts. Then there was another lightning strike, and he saw the image of *The Spider*: Rex—as clear as day, standing in his kitchen. The image disappeared when the lightning stopped, just flashed like a light switching on and off. There followed a laugh, which he now recognised as Rex's. Holding both of his ears to shut out the sound, he ran to the kitchen door, but the door slammed shut before he could get there. George stopped in his tracks and twirled around shakily. 'Wh-who are you?' he said, in a half-whisper, fear tugging at his heart. 'Wh-what do you want from me?'

'*I am the soul of The Spider.*'

'The... Th-the spider?'

'*I am The Spider,*' came Rex's voice. '*You killed me. Now I will have my revenge. I will possess the body of your next child, and I will continue my mission.*' A chilling laugh resounded and then the room became calm. The rain stopped and the storm appeared to have passed. There was nothing to prove that anything untoward had happened.

Walking out of the kitchen and up the stairs to the bedroom in a daze, George stumbled onto his bed and fell into a deep, dreamless sleep.

Chapter Fifteen

'I have something to tell you,' said Roisin at breakfast.

George was still reeling from the nightmare he'd had the night before, although he couldn't decide if it was a nightmare or reality. He'd seen the image of Rex in a spider suit as clear as day.

'What is it?' he said, hardly meeting her eyes.

'I'm pregnant,' she said.

He spat out the piece of toast that he'd just bitten, afraid he would choke. 'P-pregnant?'

'I'm as shocked as you are, but it is what it is. We're having a baby.'

Roisin had thought long and hard about it. She didn't want to have an abortion and Hugh was not a great role model for a child. From witnessing his recent behaviour, she had come to the conclusion that he was an alcoholic. Whether he had been all along and Abigail left him because of his addiction, or whether he'd become an alcoholic because Abigail left him, remained unclear. She'd decided to tell George the child was his.

'We can't have another child, Roisin; it's out of the question.' George stood up. He could hardly contain the torment in his mind. Rex's words were playing over and over: *You killed me... I will have my revenge... possess the body of your next child...'* 'You have to have an abortion,' he demanded, a bit too loudly, in an attempt to quieten the voices in his head.

Her mouth fell open. 'How can you say that? Think of little Robbie. He's the best thing that's ever happened to us. What if we'd got rid of him? Remember at the time, you thought you might lose your job and you said I should have an abortion—'

'I know, I know, but if you knew—' George paused to look around the kitchen, as if expecting to see something, as if they were being spied on. Was Rex peering down on him from some corner of the room, silently mocking him? 'We s-said we'd only... we'd only have one child, remember?' he spluttered.

Roisin's eyes widened. 'When? We'd planned to have another baby when Robbie was a bit older. Remember we used to say—'

'We can't have another child, so get it out of your head!' George slammed his fist on the kitchen table, causing Roisin to gasp.

'Sorry,' he said. Sitting down, he placed his head in his hands, elbows on the kitchen table.

Roisin touched his shoulder. 'What's wrong?' she whispered, 'Please tell me.'

He reached out and took her hands in his. 'Please, Roisin, I'm begging you, please don't have this child. There is a reason, but you wouldn't believe me if I told you.'

'What are you saying?' She took a seat next to him.

Fear emanated from his eyes.

'George?'

He looked down at the floor. 'Okay, okay. I'll tell you, but you can't judge me. You just have to believe me; we'll arrange for you to have an abortion.'

'I'm not having an abortion.'

George sighed. 'A couple of years ago, Glen and I went to a fortune teller,' he lied. 'She told me I should never have another child because it would bring bad news.'

Glaring at him, she said, 'Why haven't you told me this before?'

'I didn't believe it—didn't want to believe it—but it's still in here,' he pointed to his head, 'and we can't risk it.'

Roisin walked over to the kitchen sink; she stared out of the window for a couple of minutes and then slowly turned to face him.

He met her eyes for a painful second, then looked at the kitchen table recalling Rex's disembodied voice and the warning he'd given right here in this kitchen the night before. George struggled to find peace of mind. Surely it must have been a nightmare... How could he be believing it? Was he actually willing to force Roisin to have an abortion because of a bad dream he'd had? Perhaps it was, in some weird way, Rex's revenge from the grave: he wanted him to kill his own child. George held his head with his hands, hardly able to contain the inner turmoil.

'It seems we've both been keeping secrets from each other,' said Roisin.

George swivelled around in his chair to face her.

She closed her eyes and then returned to her seat at the table. 'This might not be... Oh, who am I kidding? This *isn't* your baby.' She held her tummy.

'What?' he blurted, suddenly alert.

'It was a brief fling.' She shook her head as if to expel her thoughts. 'It's over. If I hadn't of got pregnant—'

'Who the fuck *is he*?' boomed George, images of the handsome neighbour flashing in his mind.

Roisin looked at her hands. 'Does it matter? It's over.'

'D-do I know him?'

'No... Well, not really.'

'What does that mean?'

'It's the neighbour, okay? Hugh, the neighbour.'

He closed his eyes. 'The conniving—'

'We were drunk—' She was standing now, looking uncomfortable as if she wanted to leave the room.

'Huh!' He pointed at her. 'That's why you kept telling me you didn't like Abigail, isn't it? You were screwing her husband and she suspected, and you kept saying that you couldn't understand why she hated you; you were trying to put me off the scent.'

'No. You're being paranoid. Abigail never knew about it.'

'You're lying. So, have you and lover boy been laughing behind our backs, then?' George had seen Hugh outside his house on the way back from work, a couple of weeks earlier; he'd said hello but Hugh had just given him a half-smile and nodded. George remembered feeling sorry for the man, knowing his wife had abandoned him and taken his son. All the time, Hugh was sleeping with Roisin. His stomach churned as he now realised that he'd only found out about Abigail leaving Hugh because Roisin had told him. 'The smug git,' said George aloud as he recalled the look on Hugh's face and now believed the man had been inwardly mocking him. 'You're still seeing him, aren't you?'

'No.'

'How could you, Roisin? You blatantly broke up a marriage... Abigail left when she discovered your sordid affair, didn't she? Did she catch you at it?'

'For God's sake.' Roisin looked up at him briefly, then down at her hands. 'That's not why she left him. The day she left was the day we were meant to go there for dinner. He was upset, so I stayed because he said he needed company; he got drunk, and so did I... One thing led to another.' Her cheeks reddened. She walked to the window.

'Do you love him?'

'I don't know... No, no, of course not.'

He couldn't get the image of Hugh out of his head: the last time he saw him, he'd appeared so bedraggled, like a tramp. Did she actually prefer him?

'Why, Roisin? I thought we were happy.'

She turned to face him. 'You're to blame! You weren't

there! We were both invited to the dinner party and then the next week, but you decided not to go, and I was left alone. If I wasn't alone—'

'So, if I don't chaperone you wherever you go you'll end up sleeping with other people? Can you hear yourself? What is a marriage if there isn't trust? I trusted you!'

There was silence as they both glowered at each other.

Roisin resumed staring out of the window. 'I'm having this baby. You can either stand by me or not.'

'I can't,' he said. 'How can I ever trust you again?'

'Fine,' she said.

'So, are you gonna move in with Hugh?' he snarled. 'Is that why you're not even bothered about our marriage falling apart?'

'No! I don't love Hugh.'

'Well, you can stop fooling yourself that you love me, because if you did you wouldn't have betrayed me.'

'You're not innocent in all this, George.'

'No. Maybe not.' He looked at the floor. 'I'll give you until this evening to pack your stuff and get out.' He stood up to face her.

'Me?'

'Yes, of course. This is all your fault.'

'You can't just throw me out! What about Robbie?'

'I get to keep Robbie.'

'No, you don't! If I'm going, I'm taking him with me.'

'Hmm. I suppose he'll only be living next door; I can still see him,' said George, venom in his eyes.

'You're a bastard.'

'And, you're a whore. Nice pair we make, hey?'

Pushing him out of the way, Roisin made a beeline for the kitchen door, then looked back at him. 'Are you being serious now, George? Because when I leave this house I'm gone, and Robbie's coming with me. You'll never see me again.'

'Just fuck off.'

'Don't worry, I'm leaving. I don't want to spend another minute with you!'

'I'm filing for divorce, and I'll get custody of Robbie. No court would give you custody. You're such a great mother that you leave your son alone in the house so you can sleep with the neighbour.'

'It wasn't like that. Robbie was at Cilla's house that first time—'

Humiliation coloured his cheeks red. 'So Cilla knows? What? You've been gossiping with your sister about what a neglectful husband you have and how you have to sleep with the neighbour for fulfillment? Who else knows?'

'No one knows. Cilla doesn't know anything about—'

'And, what did you mean "that first time"? This has been going on for a while? How many times?'

'I don't know. It wasn't a regular thing.'

'You're unbelievable.'

'Go and find Glen. You spend more time with him than anyone else; have you considered that you might be gay?'

'Glen is a better friend than you'll ever be, and if I prefer spending time with him it's because he doesn't nag and blame all the time. Oh, and relationships don't revolve around sex. But I suppose a whore like you wouldn't be able to understand that.'

'Fuck you!'

George watched as she left the room, taking with her any hope of his life reverting to normal. *I am The Spider. I will win.* George couldn't be sure if the voice in his head was just him remembering Rex's threat or if he was here now, watching.

As George heard Roisin storm up the stairs, he felt a

strange and irrational sense of relief. With her no longer in his life, he couldn't have another child and *The Spider*'s threat would never have a chance to come true. At the same time, he wanted to run after her and convince her to stay so he could reclaim his life instead of watching it fall to pieces.

Chapter Sixteen

'Good for you, mate. You've finally seen sense.'

'Then why do I feel so bad?'

'You've got nothing to feel bad about. She slept with the neighbour behind your back. I'll get us another drink so you can forget about her.'

George watched as his friend walked up to the bar. It was late afternoon. Roisin had collected Robbie from school and told him she'd be taking him to stay with his grandparents for a while. She'd moved back in with her parents, who lived only five minutes away. George knew this meant he'd still see her around—perhaps even have to see her with Hugh. He would have preferred it if she left the neighbourhood or even the country, unable to bear the idea of the two of them together—happy, laughing, in love—but then he thought of Robbie; he missed him already. Living in a different house from his son was hard enough.

He decided he'd have to consult a solicitor, find out what his rights were. Robbie should be living with him. Roisin was the one who'd wrecked their marriage, getting pregnant by another man.

Running alongside these thoughts were other ones—thoughts that told him that if he split with his wife, *The Spider* will have won. Maybe this is what Rex wanted to happen. Perhaps he'd known Roisin was pregnant, so he had concocted this story about how their second born would have the soul of *The Spider*, knowing George would try to convince her to have an abortion, knowing she wouldn't agree, knowing they'd split.

'It's him,' said George as soon as Glen returned, placing a pint of beer in front of him.

'Who?' asked Glen, looking around the pub.

'The Spider. Rex.'

Glen sat opposite him and wrinkled his nose. 'That freak is dead. Forget him.'

'He's haunting me.' George stared at Glen. 'Last night he was in my house. He's the one who split me and Roisin up.'

'What're you on about? How much did you have to drink last night?' Glen chuckled.

'Don't you see? I have to get her back. Her and Robbie. If I don't, Rex will win. He wants to ruin my life.'

'Calm down.' For once, Glen didn't respond with a sharp and witty line but seemed lost for words. 'George, I think you need therapy,' he said eventually. 'You've been having all these bad dreams since that weirdo locked us up, right? You should go and talk to a professional.'

'I've had it up to here with all your wind-ups. I'm not crazy. I know what this man is trying to do.' George picked up his pint glass and drank half of the beer in one go.

'Look, Rex is dead. He can't hurt you. If you're thinking anything else, then you need help. I'm not saying you're crazy, I'm just saying you—'

'I don't need therapy! I need my wife and son back. We were fine until he came along. He was the one who engineered all of this. I wouldn't be surprised if he made Roisin sleep with Hugh. He's the one who made me go back into that house and light the match—'

'What?' Glen leaned towards him. 'What house? Rex's house? When you went back in for your phone, did you—'

'I have to go.' George drank the other half of the beer and wiped his mouth with his sleeve. 'Thanks for the drink and the chat; I can see it more clearly now. I won't let him win.'

🕷

Roisin lay on the single bed in the room that had been hers as a young girl. The walls were still painted the same dusky pink colour she had used to redecorate when she'd been into all the DIY shows on TV and fancied herself as an interior designer. A border ran across the centre of the room with pictures of cats and teddy bears on it. A child's room. *Oh, to be a child again.* If she had a time machine, she'd do things differently. A tear fell from her eye; she wiped it and chided herself. Why cry? The blame lay with her.

She imagined George lying alone in their bed, upset and thinking of her betrayal. *I shouldn't have told him.* Then she remembered why she had: it was after hearing that strange story about George seeing a fortune teller. It'd made her worry that George could be slightly unhinged. He hadn't been himself of late, didn't talk much—not about anything of substance—and had woken up in distress, screaming a few times, as if hiding a terrible secret. She'd been too afraid to ask him what was troubling him. Whenever she asked, 'Are you all right?' after being disturbed by another of his screams in the night, he'd stare at her, his eyes slightly dazed. More than once she'd worried he might be on some kind of drug.

Perhaps he'd cheated on her too. What if he wasn't seeing Glen on those nights out? Maybe they were dates with another woman. It would go some way to explaining his reaction when she'd first told him she was pregnant—wanting to get rid of the baby. Perhaps this had all worked out for the best for him now, freeing him to move in with his new lover.

Even as she pondered this, Roisin knew it couldn't be true. George would never cheat on her; loyalty was part of his DNA.

Another tear fell down her cheek, but she didn't bother to wipe it away; she liked the way it felt, waited for it to drip into her mouth, tasted the saltiness.

Robbie had screamed for his daddy a few times. Wanted him to read a bedtime story: 'Daddy always reads me stories and he makes them more fun! You don't do the funny faces and the voices,' Robbie had complained. The boy eventually cried himself to sleep.

George's threat played on her mind: he'd mentioned divorce, said he'd apply for custody of Robbie. If the court asked Robbie who he'd rather live with, he'd choose George; she was sure of that. She'd be left alone. Then she remembered the child inside her and thought about Hugh. Was it worth going to see him and explaining? Did he drink because his life was a mess? Would he stop drinking so heavily if she went and offered him some hope, a new life with her and their baby?

She rolled over on the bed and switched off the bedside lamp, falling into a deep sleep, tears still pouring from her eyes.

Chapter Seventeen

Roisin watched from the school gates as Robbie ran towards his friends. The plan had been that she'd go and talk to Hugh. He had a right to know, after all. Would he be at home?

She thought back to a few months earlier when she'd fallen for his charms. It was an option she'd considered back then, leaving George and moving in with Hugh, who'd seemed infinitely more exciting at the time.

Should she try again? Apologise to George, beg him to forgive her, promise to abort the child? Her hand went to her belly; a protective action. The only thing she was sure about was that she wanted this baby.

At the gate to Hugh's house, she looked over to the left and saw the house she'd shared with George. It had been home for so many years. Memories tumbled through her mind as she looked at the front door. The keys were in her bag. *I could go in, refuse to leave.* What could George do? Forcibly evict her? Shaking away the nostalgia, she concentrated on the reason she had come back here.

She walked up the path and confidently knocked on Hugh's front door.

He answered the door, squinting at the sun as he did so, like a man who'd been locked in a dark room. The interior of the house was shadowy, Roisin noticed, as if his mood had altered the place to match the greyness of his thoughts.

'Roisin?' His despondency visibly shifted then; his green eyes, which had of late appeared dark and tormented whenever she caught a glance when passing him in the street, now began to sparkle ever so slightly.

'Hugh,' she said, avoiding his eyes, 'can I come in?'

He opened the door wider and ushered her in with a flourish of his hand. She caught a whiff of something sour, which she assumed was his breath.

She headed straight for the living room and, without waiting to be asked, sat on the sofa.

He smiled at her as if smiling was something he never did; his face stiff, his countenance devoid of emotion.

'What can I get you to drink?' he asked.

'Don't you think you've had enough to drink, Hugh?'

'Who made you my guardian?' He went to the bar.

After pouring himself a whisky, he sat beside her. 'My only pleasure is the drink these days,' he said, looking directly into her eyes.

She averted her gaze.

'Abigail doesn't let me see Liam, you know. She says I drink too much. But she doesn't realise that I drink because I can't see my son. And she's the one who drove me to drink in the first place. I lost my job, too. Turned up late too many times, and turned up drunk another time.'

'Sorry to hear that. Listen, Hugh, if you stop drinking so much, get your life back on track, Abigail won't be able to stop you seeing Liam. You have to start making an effort.'

'Who sent you here?' He knocked back his whisky. 'Why do you care all of a sudden?'

'I'm pregnant.'

He stood up and glared at her. 'Well, whoopee. Congratulations. Is hubby pleased? You came here with your false pretences, let me have sex with you, then you go back to your perfect husband and your perfect little house, and now you're having another child. Why the hell did you think I would wanna know?'

'Stop shouting. Let me speak. The baby's yours, damn it!'

He dropped his tumbler onto the floor.

Both of them stared at it.

'It's mine?' he asked eventually.

'Yes. I thought you had a right to know.' She stood up and covered her face with her hands for a moment.

'So what do you want? Money? I can't afford to—'

'No. I thought—' She glanced at him and then shook her head again. 'Never mind.' Picking up her handbag from the sofa, she headed for the door.

'Roisin, wait.'

She stopped but didn't turn around.

'Does your husband know about us?'

'Yes.'

'So, maybe I should go and explain.'

She looked at him, tears threatening to fall. 'I already told him.'

'Great. So you're cool. Everything's cool between you two?'

'Is that what you want me to say?'

Hugh sat on the sofa, appearing sober now, despite having consumed another glass of whisky. He had a lost and distant look in his eyes. 'I need to sort my life out, Roisin. I'm losing the battle.'

She sat next to him and hung her head. 'George threw me out; I'm staying with my parents. So I guess we're both in the same boat.'

'It's because of me,' said Hugh, head down.

'No. We were both... I don't know, we both needed—'

'I've messed it up, haven't I?'

'What?'

'I'm just a sad old drunk now. Would you still want me? Remember what we said before, you know, after the last time —we were planning to get together, weren't we? I said I'd leave Abi.'

Roisin picked at her nails, nervously. 'I felt terrible for

betraying him,' she said. 'That's why I didn't want to leave him. But now he's thrown me out.'

'You still love him.'

'Um, yes. I think so. Yes, I do, but—'

'That's the difference. I don't love Abi; don't think I ever did. I could love you, though.' He touched her cheek.

She flinched.

'Wh-why did you come here?'

'To tell you about the baby.' Roisin stood up.

'You can move in with me, if you have nowhere—'

'I'm staying with my parents. I couldn't bring Robbie here, anyway. George lives next door.'

Hugh rose to face her. 'Is that the only reason?' He gazed into her eyes. 'I would do anything for you. I'll clean myself up. We can rent a place and bring up our child together.'

'I-I-I don't know.' She turned to leave.

'So you're leaving and taking my child, just like Abi did?' he shouted out behind her.

There was a melancholy tone to his voice that tore at her heart. She looked at him. 'Listen, Hugh, get yourself cleaned up, get a job, and we'll talk then. There's no way I would deny you access to the child, but... but look at you.' She pointed at him. 'You're a mess.'

'I know.' He walked towards her. 'I'll stop drinking, I promise. Then we can move in together. You, me, and the baby, right?'

'Take care, Hugh. This isn't goodbye. Don't worry. Sort yourself out.'

Her mind was a whirl of confusion as she left the house. Had she led him on unfairly? Did she really want to move in with him, start a new life with him and their child? She needed to talk to George, needed to see him.

As Roisin put the key in the lock to open the front door, tears formed in her eyes. Footsteps sounded up the path behind her and then the shadow of a tall person was outlined on the white front door. A man. She stiffened. *Hugh?* Had he followed her out of his house? Her thoughts were now clouded by anger. She needed time to think, didn't want him rushing her, forcing her to make a decision. He had to clean himself up; hadn't she spelt it out clearly enough? With all of that racing through her mind, she spun around: 'Why can't you leave me alone—' She blinked, now face to face with someone she hadn't expected to see. 'G-George? Wh-what are you doing here?'

'I live here,' he said.

Closing her eyes, she faced the door. 'I only came to collect some stuff. Don't worry, I won't be long.'

'I'm glad you're here,' he said.

She half-turned back to face him, an eyebrow raised in query.

'I was gonna come and see you,' he continued. 'We should talk.'

'Talk?' She eyed him pensively.

'Y-yes...' He bowed his head. 'I may have been a bit rash.' His brown eyes searched hers. 'I can't bear the thought of losing you. It came as a shock... finding out about...'

She finished unlocking the door. 'Thank God,' she said under her breath, realising she didn't want to lose him either. 'Let's talk.' She led the way through to the kitchen.

They sat opposite each other at the kitchen table, a pot of tea in the centre. Roisin had a flashback to when she'd been sitting like this with Hugh after the first time they'd slept together. Their kitchens were almost identical in layout, being next door in a terraced street. Once again, gut-wrenching guilt tore her up from inside.

'I'm so sorry, for everything.' She poured cups of tea for both of them, and spoke the words to smother her feelings of inadequacy. Her recent actions had astounded her: it was something she'd sworn she would never do. Her father had many affairs and her mother forgave him, time and time again; Roisin had inwardly mocked her mother, thinking her weak, and had scorned her father's behaviour, thinking him irresponsible and immature. Now she'd followed in his footsteps. Had she been destined to cheat on George? Was that how it worked, history repeating itself, lessons never learned? A sense of self-loathing brought anguish, but another part of her felt there was nothing wrong with what she'd done; as if it were an inherited pattern of behaviour. Still, it was hard to come to terms with the repercussions, the pregnancy, and the way she'd so easily betrayed George.

'I neglected you. You said so yourself. I've been thinking about what you said. It's true; I do spend too much time with my friends when I should be with you and Robbie. I'll change. I promise. Let's find a way round this.' He took his cup of tea and sipped it, not meeting her eyes.

His words were like a soothing balm to her self-deprecating thoughts. If he could forgive her for this, perhaps she'd be able to forgive herself in time. It was hope of an absolution she wanted to keep a grasp of. 'You were so angry before. I-I...'

He stared into his tea cup as if reading his fortune. 'Anger won't bring anything back, won't change anything. I need to know you still love me and we have a future.' He looked up and stared into her eyes.

No passion existed in his stare, no emotion at all, except maybe a latent fear calling out to her, indicating that perhaps he needed her to stay with him. 'I... Yes, I love you, of course I do.' She reached out a hand and took his. 'I'm so sorry. I've learned a hard lesson. I honestly don't know if I'll ever be able to forgive myself.' She blinked away a tear, then went on, 'While we're on the subject—and as I have nothing to lose—I'll tell you everything, and if you want to leave me afterwards I'll totally understand. But I have to tell you why I did it; it's been going around in my head and driving me mad.' She let go of his hand and took a tissue to dry her eyes.

'You don't have to explain,' he said. 'I was to blame as well.'

'No. I don't have any excuse for what I did. I felt unappreciated, but now I realise I made a mistake. Hugh showed me affection and—'

George stood up. 'I don't want to hear it,' he said through gritted teeth. 'What's done is done. We'll move forward.'

She wanted to say so much more, but realised that perhaps she was being selfish. George didn't need to hear it. 'Fine. But we have to talk about the baby.'

'I'll stand by you; whatever you decide.'

'I've decided to keep it. And I think Hugh will want contact by the way he was talking today.'

George raised his eyebrows. 'You saw him today?' His cheeks reddened.

Roisin averted her eyes. 'Er... I—'

'What's going on, Roisin?' He slammed his fist on the kitchen table. 'Are you still seeing him? How many more lies?'

She tentatively rose from her chair. 'Please, George, calm down. I only went to see him to tell him about the baby. He has a right to know.'

'He's a bloody drunk,' boomed George. 'I saw him last week on my way back from work; he looked like a homeless man. He was sitting on his garden wall, dirty clothes, looking like he hadn't shaved in a month, a beer can in his hand. He's a loser. His wife's left him because he's an alcoholic and has affairs.'

She looked down at the table, cheeks flushed. 'He said he's gonna clean himself up, for the baby's sake,' she said in a small voice.

'What about his son? Liam? He didn't clean himself up for him. I think we need to set some boundaries here. If we bring up this child together, I don't want Hugh involved. It's the least you can do for me.'

'But...' She was going to protest, but what was the point? Wasn't it better to agree with whatever George wanted and keep her family together? 'Fine.'

'I think we should move away from here,' George muttered.

'But Robbie's settled in to the school, he loves it here.'

'It doesn't have to be out of the neighbourhood. I just don't want to be living next door to that man. Surely you can understand that?'

She nodded.

'Good,' said George. 'I'll go to the estate agent tomorrow at lunchtime and find out what's available.'

Chapter Eighteen

George hesitated slightly before entering the house at 8 Goldfern Road. He heard the sound of machinery and builders working on the house, but there still existed an inner fear, concern about his safety, fear of *The Spider*.

'George!' called Glen from inside what had once been the living room that had housed the spinning wooden spiderweb. Now it was a mere shell; none of the original plasterwork remained. All the walls had been stripped bare.

Charred areas that reminded George of the fire could still be seen on the edges of some of the remaining woodwork.

'Hi, Glen, I didn't expect to see you here.'

'I didn't expect to see you, either. What're you doing here?'

'Just popped in. I went to the estate agents. I was on my way back to work, but thought I'd make a detour.'

'It doesn't look like much at the moment,' said Glen looking up at the ceiling, 'but the builders are making good progress. I just popped in too. Curiosity, I suppose. Can't wait to see the end result.' He rubbed his hands together.

A tall man with ruddy cheeks, dressed in overalls and wearing a builders' cap approached them. 'Glen.'

'Hi, Jack. This is George, my best friend. Don't think you two have met, have you?'

George shook his head and extended a hand to Jack, who nodded at him apologetically and held up his hands that were covered in dust. 'Nice to meet you.' Then to Glen, he said, 'You'll have to leave now, I'm afraid; we're about to start work in here.'

'No problem, I have to get back to work.'

As Glen and George stepped outside they saw Lisa leaving her house.

'Hi guys!' she said, waving her arms and running over to them.

'We're in a hurry,' said Glen, rushing along the garden path.

Lisa's mouth fell into a sulk as she watched him leave.

George acknowledged her and said, 'Sorry, I have to get back to work. Nice seeing you again.'

She glanced at him and smiled, then looked back at Glen, who was now a few doors down. 'Have I done anything to offend him?' she asked.

'Who? Glen? No, he's generally a miserable bastard.' George chuckled.

Lisa joined in the laughter, her gaze still fixed on Glen in the distance.

George ran after Glen, 'Hey, even for your standards that was a bit rude,' he said, panting.

'What was?'

'That.' He pointed back at the house. Lisa was no longer there. 'You could have at least said hello to the girl. She has a crush on you.'

'When you're as handsome as I am, everyone has a crush on you.'

'Huh!'

'Seriously, mate. She's a bit creepy. Whenever I go to the house she's somehow there. She goes in and offers tea to the builders and flutters her eyelashes at me. I'm a bit sick of it, to be honest.'

'She's only being friendly.'

'It doesn't matter, anyway, 'cos Matt—one of the builders—has a crush on her, I think. He blushes when she speaks to him. Hopefully they'll end up together.'

'She only has eyes for you.'

'She's one step away from being a stalker; that's why I've resorted to being rude. I need her to get the message that I'm not interested.'

'Who are you interested in?'

Glen stood still and folded his arms. 'Do I have to be interested in someone? Can't I just be me?'

'Yeah, you can, but since you split with Georgia—what was it now, two years ago?—you haven't even looked at another woman. You've got to get out there. You're not still pining over her, are you?'

'No.'

'No, because you're still pining over Petula.'

'What would you know about it?'

'I know that you fell in love with a girl who clearly didn't feel the same way about you—'

'She loved me too.'

'Yeah, for five minutes, twenty years ago, and you can't forget her. It's like you're delusional.'

'It was fifteen years ago, actually.'

'She's not coming back.'

'I've had loads of relationships since Petula,' protested Glen.

'Yeah, but none of them have worked out.'

'I like to spread my net wide.'

'It's time you looked for a woman to settle down with. You need to think of commitment.'

Glen started walking again, in the direction of the high street. 'Why? So I can be lied to all over again?'

'Not all women are the same.'

'I'm surprised you're so positive about women considering what Roisin did.'

'We're trying to put it behind us.'

Glen put an arm out to stop George walking further.

'You two are back together? When did that happen?'

'Yesterday.'

'I can't believe it.'

'It's called being an adult. Relationships are hard, you have to take the good with the bad. We've got a kid to think about.'

'I'd rather be single than in a relationship with someone I can't trust.'

'Whatever.'

'Let's change the subject. Have you had lunch yet?' Glen stopped outside the local pub.

'Yes.' George looked at his watch. 'I'd better get back to work.'

Glen shrugged and they headed towards the Tube station. 'Did you say you went to the estate agent earlier?'

'Yeah, I was—'

'Checking out the house prices? Yeah, I've been doing that.' Glen smiled. 'I think we can get a great price for the place when it's been renovated.'

'No, I wasn't there because of the house. Me and Roisin are selling up and moving on.'

'Moving?'

'Yeah, still in the same area, but we want to move.'

'I can't believe you two are back together.' He blinked exaggeratedly. 'And you have the nerve to try and give *me* relationship advice.'

'We have to do what's best for Robbie,' mumbled George.

'I can definitely see why you'd wanna move away. Temptation is there every day for Roisin with the hunky neighbour living next door.'

'It's not like that. She isn't seeing him anymore.'

'Is that what she told you?'

'We're gonna make a fresh start. We want to leave what

happened behind us.'

'Good luck with that,' said Glen, running a hand through his hair. 'Pity you can't live at old Rex's house when it's been done up, but that'd defeat the point. We have to try and get lots of money for it so we can celebrate on an exotic holiday.'

George felt a shiver. 'I wouldn't want to live there, anyway. Way too spooky.'

'Ghosts are just ghosts, mate. They belong in the past and that's where the freaky spider is staying. Don't let it get to you.'

'You're right,' said George, knowing he couldn't shift the fear and anxiety, wondering if he'd ever be free.

Chapter Nineteen

Roisin arrived home after collecting Robbie from school. The child ran up to his room straight away.

As soon as she'd closed the front door, the doorbell rang. She looked through the spyhole and was surprised to see Hugh. Should she open the door? He must have seen her enter the house—there was no point trying to pretend she wasn't at home. Would he leave if she didn't answer the door, or would he insist on seeing her? If he was drunk he might even make a scene.

He'd been sitting on his garden wall, drinking from a can, as she left the house to collect Robbie and she'd ignored him, even though he'd lifted his can in the air and said, 'Roisin, cheers.' She mostly avoided looking in his direction whenever she passed him; she needed to work on putting the pieces back together with George, didn't want any distractions.

He had not been outside when she'd returned with Robbie, so she'd forgotten about him. Almost. He was always there at the back of her mind, as much as she tried to forget him; like a story that needed an ending. It had been a month since she'd told him about the pregnancy.

Hesitating, she opened the door.

Hugh greeted her with a smile.

'H-Hugh... wh-what are you doing here?'

'Just came to say hello. Can I come in?'

'Um... Robbie's at home.'

'I promise I won't seduce you into sex on the sofa.' He grinned.

She felt the strong pull of attraction and hated herself for it. He was more like his old self: he'd shaved, had a hair cut, dressed smartly. Despite a voice in her head screaming *no*, she opened the door wider and gestured for him to enter.

Once in the front room, he sat on the sofa.

The smell of his aftershave brought back guilty memories. He looked nothing like the bedraggled and forlorn man she had chatted to last month. She stood by the side of the sofa. 'Can I get you something to—' She stopped herself.

'Don't worry,' he said, 'I've given up the drink. I'm working hard to become a better man. I want to show you that I am. It means everything to me that you trust me to be able to do that, and I'm holding on to the hope of me and you and our baby sharing happier times. I've even got a job interview. Next week. It's with a bank.'

She felt terrible, recalling how when she told him about the baby, she'd said that if he cleaned himself up she might reconsider their relationship. Things had changed.

She sat next to him. 'Um, Hugh... you have to understand that I'm trying to save my marriage, do what's best for Robbie.'

Hugh took her hand and leaned closer to her. 'Please don't forget what we talked about before. You're not happy with George; you know that. If you'd been happy with him, you wouldn't have slept with me behind his back. It wasn't only once, was it? You kept coming back. Is that the behaviour of a woman who wants to save her marriage? Ask yourself.'

Roisin pulled her hand away and averted her eyes. 'It was different then.'

'In what way?' He touched her cheek softly and turned her face towards him.

Looking into his green eyes, she was overcome. He didn't seem to be drunk. Had he sorted his life out? For her? How romantic. To think she was someone's reason for going on, someone's light in the darkness.

Her life with George was far from perfect, with the

constant feeling that he was judging her for the affair, that he'd never completely forgiven her.

She placed her head in her hands, confused. How could this man hold such power over her when she knew he was lying?

Sitting up, Roisin confronted him: 'Hugh, if you are trying to give up the booze, I think that's great, I really do. But, I saw you.'

'Saw me? I'm not sure I know what you mean.'

'You were sitting on your garden wall when I went to collect Robbie from school and you had a beer can in your hand. You said "cheers" as I went by, remember?'

'Beer? No. That was coke.'

'Coke?'

'Yeah! You don't believe me? Come and see. I left it in my kitchen.'

'But Robbie's upstairs. I can't leave him here.'

'It's only next door.' Hugh took her hand.

She followed him out of the door and into his house. He led her to the kitchen and showed her a can on the edge of the worktop. A soft-drink can. She couldn't be sure if it was the one he'd been holding. Her brow creased into a frown as she tried to remember. Perhaps she'd expected to see a beer can in his hand because she believed he was an alcoholic.

'I'm sorry, Hugh. I'm so sorry for accusing you.'

'That's okay, honey, I understand why you did.'

Honey?

His emerald-green eyes were reeling her in again. She wanted him to kiss her, but knew it was wrong. *Was it?* Hadn't George driven her into his arms before? And now he expected her to move, leave the home she loved. It was always about what *he* wanted.

Hugh moved closer and took her in his arms. 'I've

missed you,' he whispered.

Roisin put her arms around him. *What am I doing?*

He leaned back and smiled. 'I won't let you down. You and I, we married the wrong people, but somehow fate has intervened. What are the chances that you'd be living right next door to me? My perfect woman. Now we're having a child and I couldn't be happier. You've breathed new life into me, brought me back from the edge. You know, I had even thought of ending it all many times, but you... you saved me, Roisin. You saved me.' Leaning in, he kissed her full on the mouth.

She found herself returning his kiss. His words played back in her mind. He'd been in an unhappy marriage; driven to drink; considered "ending it all"; she'd "saved him". She pulled away from his embrace. It was too much of a burden to bear, being responsible for making sure he didn't kill himself. What if she failed to make him happy? Would she be the one to drive him to drink next time? But she couldn't dump him, not right now; that would ensure he'd be back on the drink again and she'd be to blame. And, he was the father of the child growing inside her. The child needed a father.

Somehow, when she was in Hugh's arms, George became a secondary character; unimportant. Hugh made her feel young again.

She hated herself for betraying George, but Hugh kissed her again and suddenly it didn't matter.

'We'll escape.' He nuzzled against her neck. 'I know you're worried about your husband finding out.' He leaned back and looked at her, his eyes burning with passion. 'We were meant to be together. Leave him. We'll go away. Far away. None of them will be able to find us.'

Freeing herself from his hold, she made her way to the kitchen door. 'It's all dreams, Hugh. You have a son and I have a son. We can't abandon them. Oh, my God.' She placed a hand over her mouth. 'Robbie is all alone in there!' She ran towards the front door and grabbed the latch.

Hugh followed, taking hold of her breasts from behind, pulling her close to him. 'You know we should be together, Roisin. I love you,' he whispered.

She felt aroused and unable to resist his kiss, but forced herself to wriggle out of his arms. 'I have to go to Robbie.'

He nodded. 'I know. Come back later.'

'I-I—'

His eyes beckoned.

She knew she would be back.

Chapter Twenty

'She's sleeping with the neighbour.'

The whisper sounded in the still of the night, waking George from a restless sleep.

'She's sleeping with the neighbour,' the voice repeated, directly into his ear like a bothersome mosquito.

George sat up in bed. The streetlight shone through the bedroom window, casting a faint light into the room. Roisin wasn't in bed beside him.

Switching on the bedside lamp, he waited. Maybe she'd gone to the bathroom, or to the kitchen to get a glass of water.

'Go next door,' the whisperer insisted.

'Wh-who are you?' George shivered.

'I am The Spider. You ruined my life, now I'm ruining yours. The Spider always wins. Your wife is with the neighbour and guess who sent her there?'

George switched off the bedside lamp and tried to shut out the darkness and thoughts of his dream. *It must have been a dream,* he assured himself.

His nightmares hadn't become any easier to cope with. Too stubborn to visit a doctor, he'd kept it to himself, hadn't told Roisin. He didn't tell her about Rex or that the sale proceeds were bequeathed to him and Glen. It felt like more of a curse than a blessing.

Closing his eyes, he drifted off to sleep, wanting to block out his doubts about Roisin. It was all in his head, surely. He'd felt jealous of Hugh ever since she'd confessed she was carrying his child, but she swore she wouldn't see him again. He needed to hold on to that, didn't want to go next door and be proved wrong. His life with Roisin and Robbie was the only sane thing he had left. He could not lose his grip on that.

'What's wrong?' asked Roisin, poking her head through the kitchen doorway. 'Can't sleep?'

'No.' George was seated by the table staring out at the night sky through the window. When she entered the room, he looked at her.

'Is it those nightmares again?' she asked, frowning.

How does she know about the nightmares?

'C'mon George, you've been fidgeting in your sleep for months, screaming out loud and waking me up.'

His eyes widened. 'R-really? Um... I didn't want to worry you, so I didn't tell you I was having nightmares. It's nothing.' Staring at his hands, he mumbled, 'I've been stressed at work, that's all.'

Roisin touched his shoulder. 'D'you want to talk?'

'No.'

'You sure?'

He glanced up at her, a downturned smile on his face. 'I used to have nightmares as a child, the stress must've brought them on again.'

She leaned down and peered at him, squinting. 'What's that? You've got something black on your forehead.'

Standing up, he went over to the hallway mirror. In his reflection the tiniest black circle glinted from his forehead. He attempted to wipe it away but saw his hand through the black thing, as if it were an eye. *How can that be?*

Unable to believe it, he moved his hand up and down in front of the black shiny circle. He gulped and looked down at his hand, seeing a thin, downy, feathery strand stuck to his skin. As he tried to pull it off, he had the sinking feeling that somehow this antennae-like protrusion had become a part of him. Trying to remove it was like trying to remove part of his skin; it caused him pain and, oddly, he felt the sensation of his fingers on the strand.

I must be dreaming. I'm just tired. He trundled up the stairs and went back to bed.

The next morning, when George woke up, he recalled the weird events of the night before. Freeing his arm from under the sheet, he checked his hand and was relieved there were no feathery strands. Hesitantly, he moved a hand slowly over his forehead. The "eye" had gone. Letting out a sigh, he went to double-check in the bathroom mirror. The strange black circle had indeed disappeared. 'I was only imagining it.'

He hoped it *had* been a bad dream and not a waking incident, fearing for the state of his mental health. The police had offered him counselling after the traumatic events at 8 Goldfern Road, but he didn't take up the offer. A stab of regret assailed him. The dreams were becoming more terrifying and more realistic. He wished he could be more like Glen. Nothing fazed Glen.

'Are you all right, George?' Yawning, Roisin entered the en-suite.

'Yeah, yeah, fine.'

'You were tossing and turning so much last night I feel a bit seasick.' She giggled.

'Sorry.'

'No, it's fine. At least you actually slept through last night. Your sleep patterns are so erratic lately, are you stressed at work?' She picked up her toothbrush. 'You look tired.'

'Um, maybe that has something to do with my wife carrying another man's child. How can you be so blasé about it?' He turned around to face her.

She lowered her eyes. 'I'm not. But we've been over it and over it. Are you going to keep bringing it up? I thought you'd forgiven me, but you obviously haven't.'

'Sorry,' he said, walking towards the bathroom door.

'George,' she shouted after him, 'I don't see how we'll ever move on if you keep holding that over my head. I've said I'm sorry, what else do you want?'

'Where were you last night?' he asked, looking at her reflection in the bathroom mirror.

She averted her gaze and spat her toothpaste into the sink. 'I was here,' she said, reaching behind him to take a towel from the towel-rail.

'I woke up and you weren't here,' he said, 'and then later when I went down for a drink you came home... It was the middle of the night.'

'You must have been dreaming. I was here all night. If I went out of the room at all it was only to Robbie's room. He was crying last night and I had to go to him.'

'Oh.' He leaned against the door frame.

'You've got to start trusting me again.'

'Yes, I know. Anyway,' he said twisting around, 'that weird black mark has gone now.'

'What black mark?' She followed him out of the en-suite.

'Last night when you found me in the kitchen and you saw that mark on my head. I could have sworn I saw my hand through it. I went like this.' He raised his hand in front of his forehead. 'I could see my hand through that black mark on my forehead. Weird, huh?'

'I didn't find you in the kitchen last night. Sounds like a weird dream.' She hugged him from behind and said, 'Listen, at least you were dreaming and not having a nightmare or sleepless night, and it's nice you were dreaming of me.' She smiled and kissed his cheek.

'Yeah, s'pose,' he said. *What's happening to me?*

Chapter Twenty-One

Roisin felt terrible about lying to George, but somehow her desire to be with Hugh was now irrepressible. She found herself sneaking out at night when George slept, to make the most of any time she could spend with her lover. The night before had been a close call; when she got back, she found George in the kitchen and she had to lie to him in the morning. He didn't seem to suspect anything, yet a part of her wished he'd discover her infidelity so that all the sneaking around could end.

The nights she spent with Hugh made her feel free. He said he loved her and told her she was beautiful. George used to say things like that in the past. Not anymore.

Hugh kept his promise. He'd given up the drink and seemed much happier. He'd been successful at the job interview and would be starting a new position at a bank in Surrey imminently. He'd be moving at the weekend and had asked her to go with him. Roisin had agreed.

Perhaps her marriage had been but one chapter in her life and it was time to move on. As hard as she tried, she couldn't imagine herself living with George and being content for the next thirty or forty years, or however long they had left to live. The affair with Hugh heralded a new phase, an exciting one, a chance to start again.

It was becoming harder to lie to George, and she often found herself feigning affection, perhaps due to guilt. She knew, deep down, it would make it more difficult for him to let go of her now that she was being so nice to him.

The worst part was leaving Robbie, but he was his father's son. He constantly cried for his daddy. It was for the best. She'd miss him dreadfully, but resolved to ask George if she could have him for the weekends.

'How are things between you and Roisin now?' asked Glen, as George sat opposite him in the pub.

'Much better,' said George. 'I think we can get through this.'

'You're a better man than me, mate. I would have sent her packing with the neighbour, maybe before or after I'd shot him.'

'What's done is done,' said George, into his beer glass. 'D'you want another drink?'

'Yeah, thanks.'

'I still can't believe you're willing to bring up that man's child as your own,' said Glen, when George returned with the beers.

Sitting down, George said, 'If I don't, I lose Roisin.'

'You should think about it. She's cheated on you once, who's to say she won't do it again?'

'I trust her.'

Tom and Jess joined them.

'Hey guys, what's up? I see you've already bought your drinks,' said Tom. 'Very nice of you.'

'Your fault if you're late,' said Glen.

Tom went to get drinks for himself and Jess.

'So, what have you two been up to since we last saw you?' said Tom, on returning from the bar.

'How are things going with the spooky house?' asked Jess.

By coincidence, they were all seated in the same seats they'd been in when George had first brought up the subject of 8 Goldfern Road.

'Can't believe you guys went into that house. Glad I didn't go,' said Tom. 'That man sounded like a loony.'

'You'll be kicking yourselves when the place is sold and me and George split the profits.'

'What? So you aren't planning to give us any of the money?' said Jess.

'Why should we?' said Glen. 'We risked our lives in there.'

Jess put on a sulky face.

'We've been friends for ages. Doesn't that count for anything?'

'Sorry Tom-Tom. Never mix business with pleasure; isn't that what they say?'

Jess rolled her eyes. 'Cheapskate.'

'Er... who's the one that's been buying you drinks all these years, with you and Tom-Tom crying poor?'

'Now we know where we stand. C'mon, Jess, we're leaving.'

'You don't have to be like that. Glen's only having a laugh.'

'Let them leave, George, if they're that two-faced. The fact that they're leaving shows they were only interested in us because they thought they'd get something from us. Now we're no use to them so they're leaving. Bang goes twenty years of friendship. We don't need false friends. We're fine on our own. Especially now we have loadsa money.'

'Who are the false friends?' accused Tom. 'Friends help each other; they don't forget about each other when they come into money.'

'Who says we're forgetting about you?' said George.

'Don't waste your time on them, George. You're too kind-hearted. They don't deserve anything.'

'Enjoy your riches, traitors,' said Tom.

'I hope you choke on it,' sneered Jess as she followed Tom out of the pub.

'Ignore them, they're jealous,' said Glen, tutting.
　'D'you think we should give them some money?'
　'Why?'
　'They are kind of poor.'
　'So? Look, it's not our problem. We went into the house. Nearly died. This is our reward. It left you with post-traumatic stress; I'd say that's worth a bit of compensation, isn't it?'
　George shrugged. 'I suppose. I still have nightmares. Last night I thought I was turning into a spider.'
　'You've always been a bit strange though, ain't you, George?' Glen wiped his mouth on his sleeve.
　'Oh, shut up. It was one of those dreams where you're so sure it's happening—'
　'Lurid dreams?'
　'Lucid.' George laughed.
　'Yeah, that's it.'
　'It freaked me out. I dreamt I was growing more eyes, and my hands were furry like a spider.'
　'Spiders don't have hands!' Glen laughed.
　'You know what I mean, my hands were feathery.'
　'Sure you weren't turning into a bird?' Glen burst out laughing and accidentally sprayed his friend's face with beer.
　'Birds don't have hands, either.' George chuckled and wiped his face with a napkin from the table. 'Anyway, it wasn't a bird, it was definitely a spider. It just seemed so real, that's all I'm saying.'
　'Blimey, it really affected you, didn't it? Look, mate, I know how you feel, but you've got to leave the past behind.'
　'But I keep having those dreams.'
　'You need time to get over it. It was pretty trippy. I

don't blame you for getting worked up. I s'pose you've got more to lose than I have, being a dad an' everything.'

'Yeah, maybe.'

'Oh, yeah, did I tell you that the solicitor told me there's been an offer on the house?'

'What? I didn't even know the builders had finished yet.'

'They're doing the finishing touches, but I thought it'd be best to let the executors get the agents in early. It's a local property investor. He's very keen, apparently.'

'I tell you what, I'll be glad to see the back of that place.'

'I dunno, you know; I've grown quite fond of it.' Glen's eyes had a wistful look about them.

'Yeah, well, you're weird.'

'Said the man who thought he was changing into a spider.'

'Ha, ha. Want another pint?'

'Yeah, go on then.'

The two friends spent a pleasant evening in the pub and left a little worse for wear.

'Roisin'll kill me,' said George, seeing that it was after 11 p.m.

'Huh!' exclaimed Glen, 'She'll be fine, probably cosying up with the next-door neighbour. While the cat's away...' He winked at George, who proceeded to push him, causing him to fall against a parked car.

'What'd'ya do that for?' snapped Glen, picking himself up and wobbling back towards George, trying to walk in a straight line.

George glared at him.

'I was only joking. I didn't think—'

'Yeah, that's your problem! You never think.

Everything's a joke to you!'

Glen suddenly appeared more sober. 'Let's go and talk about it,' he said, tugging at his friend's arm.

George pulled away to loosen Glen's grip.

They went to Glen's flat, across the road from the pub.

After fumbling in his pocket for his keys, Glen was successful in unlocking his front door on the second attempt. 'Come in, mate. I'll make us a cup of black coffee.'

On entering the flat, George nearly tripped on a beer can that was lying on the floor in the hallway. He kicked it and went into the living room. He moved some old newspapers, and junk mail that appeared to have been opened and then thrown onto the sofa.

'You live like a pig,' he said a few minutes later when Glen returned to the room holding two cups of coffee.

'I tidy up when I'm expecting guests. How was I to know you'd need emergency counselling at midnight?'

After kicking an empty pizza box off the armchair, he sat down and handed George a cup of coffee.

'So, let me get this straight, you and Roisin are back together, and you're cool about bringing up the neighbour's kid, yet you nearly killed me when I mentioned it just now. Something's not right.'

'I didn't nearly kill you.'

'If that car weren't parked there I would've fallen into the road, and if there'd been a passing car I would'a been dead.'

'You're so dramatic.'

'Yeah, I used to want to be an actor. Always fancied myself as one. But we're not talking about me now. I wanna know why you reacted like that.'

George looked up at him. 'One of the nightmares got me thinking. She might still be seeing him.'

'If you don't trust her, it won't work out. You are gonna

end up hating her, and in ten years' time you'll look back on your life and think you've wasted it bringing up another man's kid.'

George sipped his coffee and then spat it out. 'What is this shit?'

'It's instant. What d'you expect, freshly ground coffee? Sorry, you'll have to wait until the old geezer's house is sold.'

'It tastes like dishwater.'

'You drink dishwater then, do you?'

George wrinkled his nose. 'I don't know how you can drink it like this.'

'Snob. It's good enough for me.' Glen sipped his coffee and spat it out, wiping his mouth with his sleeve. 'Sorry, I forgot to boil the kettle.' He stood up. 'I'll go and—'

'I don't want coffee, I'm tired. I'm going home.'

'Think about what I said,' said Glen, following him out of the flat. 'You've gotta do what's best for you, or you'll never be happy. She's the one who betrayed you.'

George stepped outside into the cold night air. 'Yes, but what if it's all my fault?'

'You think you drove her to have an affair with him? Why? Weren't you sleeping together? Did you have problems... you know, down there?'

'No.' He looked into Glen's eyes. 'What if Rex is doing this as revenge?'

'Rex? I don't follow... I'm a bit too drunk to make sense of this.'

'I think Rex is trying to ruin my life and he wants to kill me.'

Glen began to laugh.

'Oh, I'm glad you find it funny.'

George walked away.

'Wait! It was a joke, right? George!'

Roisin sat in the kitchen watching the second hand go around the clock again. It was almost midnight. Usually she would have managed to sneak out by this time to meet Hugh. He would be wondering where she was.

Her phone sounded to alert her that she'd received a text message:

Where r u?

It was from Hugh.

R: Waiting for George to get home, he's late

H: Come over, I need you

R: I'll be over as soon as he gets back and goes to bed

H: Are u gonna tell him tonight?

R: Maybe

H: Please tell him then we can be together, no more hiding and sneaking around

R: Robbie's asleep. I have to tell him in the morning so I can take Robbie with me

H: I thought you were leaving Robbie with him

R: I am, but I have to explain to Robbie. I can't just abandon him

H: You can explain later. Just leave him

The front door opened.

George walked into the kitchen. 'Sorry, I—'

'I'm leaving you, George.'

'B-but... I'm sorry. I got carried away, had a few too many drinks.'

'You're not listening to me,' said Roisin, still sitting at the kitchen table staring at him. 'I'm leaving you. We can't go on like this. I don't love you anymore. I love Hugh.'

'No, Roisin, you can't leave me: it's not you, it's The

Spider; he's making you do this.'

'The spider is making me do this? Are you mad? Exactly how much have you had to drink?'

George stood still in the middle of the kitchen, feeling naked.

Roisin hurried past him. 'Bye, George. I'm moving away with Hugh; he's got a job in Surrey, wants me to go with him.'

'You're moving to Surrey? You're not taking Robbie!'

'Don't worry, I'm not taking him immediately. I'll take him at the weekends to begin with. He's settled in school here so it doesn't make sense to uproot him. I'm sorry. We both knew it was over.'

He watched as she left, unable to speak.

When the front door slammed shut a voice sounded: *'I've got you in my web. I'll never let you win.'*

Chapter Twenty-Two

George met Glen at 8 Goldfern Road the next day. Glen had called him to relay the news that the property investor had confirmed he would purchase the property.

'I've bought a bottle of champagne so we can celebrate the sale,' Glen had said on the phone. 'This'll be our last chance to see the place. The builders did a fantastic job; it looks great, and we got top dollar. Meet you there at lunchtime.'

George felt the same anxiety he always did on entering the house. The single positive factor today was that at last they'd sold it: perhaps with the sale of the property the nightmares would fade away too, he could only hope.

'It still feels creepy in here,' said George, peering around the living room shiftily.

'Never mind that, what'd'ya think of the place; great, isn't it?'

George looked around him; if he'd known nothing of the house's history, he'd have been tempted to put in an offer himself. 'They've done a brilliant job.'

'They have. A few finishing touches left and it'll be as good as new.' Glen popped open the champagne, and poured a glass for his friend.

George took a sip. 'Dunno if I should be drinking champagne on an empty stomach,' he said.

'Live dangerously,' said Glen. 'C'mon, let's go and have a wander around.'

They spent fifteen minutes admiring the freshly renovated house. It bore no resemblance to the dark and spooky place they'd been held captive in. Even the basement was habitable and bright.

'I could move in here myself,' said Glen. He took George's glass and refilled it.

They clinked their glasses together.

'Here's to the future and lots of money!' toasted Glen. 'The sky's the limit for us now. We'll get about five hundred thousand each.'

'Wh-what's that on your forehead?' Flashes from his recent dream taunting him, George stepped closer to his friend. 'It's like an eye—a black eye; like in my dream. Can you see my hand?' He waved it in front of the "eye".

'Course I can, you plonker.'

'No, through the eye. Close your actual eyes.' He waved a hand in front of Glen's forehead again.

'Stop it, George, you're a freak.'

Just then, a black spindly spike began to sprout from Glen's head and more "eyes" appeared.

George took a few steps backwards. 'I think you're turning into a spider. It must be what my dream meant.'

'What the hell are you on about, mate? Wouldn't have guessed you were the sort of man to take drugs. Takes all sorts.'

Glen continued to transform.

'I'm being serious. Look in the mirror. You're starting to resemble the spider-man geezer.'

'You were right about champagne on an empty stomach; you're plastered.' Glen's voice sounded strange, as if it were coming from miles away through some kind of speaker system—almost robotic. 'Get out of my way.' He stomped over to the hallway mirror. Once in front of it, he gasped and took a few steps back; then—leaning in towards the mirror—he said, in a squeaky voice that didn't sound human, 'What're all these black—' His focus shifted to his hands and the feathery down that had started to sprout: 'What's this?' Glen looked at George and gulped.

'I don't know what's happening.' George checked his own reflection as paranoia took hold, and caught his breath in relief.

He turned his attention back to the spider-like creature that had once been Glen, watching in horror as it shrank before his eyes. Glen—or whatever had possessed him—was practically dissolving, at first slowly, but then appeared to crumble; flashes and sparks of dust whizzed around him.

When George looked down at the floor he saw a large spider about three or four inches in diameter.

George screamed loudly.

They'd left the front door on the latch when they entered. Through the door came Theo the neighbour.

'What's going on in here?' asked the old man. 'I heard a scream, was that you?'

'Yeah... he... Glen...' He pointed to the arachnid.

'A spider?' said Theo, first with a confused frown, then his face brightened and he burst into a belly laugh. 'You're afraid of this little spider? That's what the screaming was about?'

George tried to open his mouth to protest when Theo lifted his foot, but no sound came out.

Theo stomped on the spider. 'There you go, son; perhaps I can get back to my lunch now.' He laughed again. 'By the way, this place looks great. I had a look around the other day when the builders were here. Are you all right, son? You're a bit pale.'

'Er... yes, fine.'

'I thought I saw you come in with your friend Glen?'

George could feel the perspiration on his brow. 'He... He had to go.'

'Well, feel free to come next door when you're finished here,' said Theo. 'Great to see you again.'

'Yes. You too.' George watched as the old man left the

house.

'*Seeing is believing but is all you see really true?*' came a familiar voice: the voice of *The Spider.* '*I've got you in my web.*'

Shivering, George kept his eyes averted, not wanting to see what remained on the floor. Shortly, he heard footsteps on the stairs.

'Right, time to go,' said Glen. 'I've gotta get back to work. So do you, I think.'

'Er... Yeah... um.. yes.' Spinning around, George saw Glen.

'Luckily, once we get the money from this place we can leave our jobs, right?' Glen was grinning as he stepped off the staircase. 'It's not for much longer!'

George reached out and hugged his friend, holding on to him as tightly as he could, tears in his eyes.

Glen pulled away. 'You're suffocating me. Look, I'm happy about it too, but no need to go all soppy on me.'

George shook his head.

He followed Glen out of the door.

Chapter Twenty-Three

In the evening, Glen called George and asked him to join him at the pub.

'I can't. I have to put Robbie to bed.'

'Come after.'

'Can't.'

'Why not? Tomorrow then?'

'Lunchtime?'

'No, in the evening. I don't wanna get the reputation of some old geezer who drinks in the pub alone every night.'

'What about Tom and Jess, ain't they there?'

'They're not talking to me.'

'Oh.'

'Come on. See you after you put Robbie to bed, yeah?'

'No, sorry.'

'What? Has Roisin put you on a curfew?'

'She's left me.'

'What?'

'Ran off with the next-door neighbour.'

'I thought that was over.'

'No. She chose him. Probably 'cos she's having his baby.'

'Wow. I had no idea. Well, that's all the more reason for you to join me, to drown your sorrows.'

'I have to look after Robbie.'

'Shall I come over there, then?'

'Okay. In an hour.'

'So, she really left you? You should've dumped her when you found out about the affair. Bitch. You're well rid.' Glen pursed his lips and poured a whisky for himself and George.

'I'm not sure I should be drinking, I have to stay alert in case Robbie wakes up.'

'Just the one, mate. You need it.'

Exhaling loudly, George took the proffered glass.

'I'm surprised she left Robbie here.'

'She'll be having him on the weekends. She didn't want to disrupt his school life.'

Glen nodded.

'If I tell you something, Glen, will you keep it between us? I haven't got my head around it yet and it's bothering me.'

'Yeah, sure.'

George lowered his gaze to stare at the coffee table. They were sitting together on the sofa in the living room.

'I think Rex is behind it.' He looked around the room as if expecting to see the man somewhere hiding behind the furniture.

'Right. Didn't I tell you that you should see a counsellor? I think you're having a hard time getting over being captured and then the fire.' He leaned towards George. 'What exactly happened in the house when you went in again, before the fire?' He narrowed his eyes.

'I poured petrol over Rex and his criminal buddies, and I lit a match and ran. I wanted to make sure he didn't escape. I was only protecting us... All of us.' George's eyes were wide.

'I knew it!' said Glen. 'You know what all this is then.'

George followed Glen's hands as he made a circle.

'What?'

'It all makes sense,' continued Glen, smiling. 'You're feeling guilty. You're a good man. You have nothing to feel guilty about: the man was a psycho. He was willing to kill us. You're a hero. Here, we'll drink a toast to you.' He held up his glass.

'It's nothing to do with feeling guilty. The man is

146

around. Do you believe in ghosts?'

'No.'

'I have proof he's still around, and he's trying to ruin my life. In fact, that's what he told me: that it's his mission to ruin my life. He even said that he was the one who made Roisin fall for the neighbour and have an affair with him.'

'This is all a bit too far-fetched, mate. Sorry. What *proof* do you have?'

'I've heard his voice, and... and he turned you into a spider. Theo came in and stepped on you but then you somehow came down the stairs, when we were in the house this morning.'

'You've lost me. Turned me into a spider?'

'Yeah, you were growing extra eyes and legs, and then you shrank.'

'Do you take drugs? I wouldn't hold it against you. I'd understand. I mean, after what happened with Rex, and then your wife leaving you; it's enough to send the sanest person off the rails.'

George stood up. 'You don't believe me and you're not listening to me; there's no point discussing it.'

'No, there isn't. Look, sit down and we'll have another drink. I brought a DVD round. Shawshank Redemption. It's a brilliant film.'

'Yeah, I saw it years ago.'

'Shall we watch it? It'll take you out of yourself.'

George shrugged and slid back down onto the sofa.

'And, don't take this the wrong way, but I really think you should go and see a counsellor, a psychiatrist. They might be able to help.'

'Yeah,' mumbled George. 'What am I supposed to say? I killed three men so they wouldn't kill us and now I think one of them is taking revenge as a ghost?'

'Sounds weird, but they hear a lot of weird stuff. It's

their job.'

'Just put the movie on. I'll deal with this my own way.'

Glen went over to the DVD player. 'By the way, I got a wedding invite recently—didn't mention it before because I wasn't sure whether I could be bothered to go. Guess who it's from.'

'Petula?'

'Ha, ha. I'll ignore that.'

'Who then?'

'It's from one of my builder mates who was working on the house.'

'Oh.'

'Guess who he's marrying.'

'Do I know her?'

'Lisa. The girl from six Goldfern Road. So you can stop winding me up now about her fancying me.'

'She did fancy you.'

'Yeah, whatever. Look, d'you wanna come along to the wedding? I can bring a guest.'

'What about Robbie?'

'I don't wanna take Robbie. I wouldn't be able to swear or have a drink. You'd be much better company.' Glen winked.

'Ha, ha!' George rolled his eyes.

'The wedding's on a Sunday; won't Roisin have Robbie then?'

'Yeah, I s'pose.'

'Great, so you'll come along?'

'Yeah, why not?'

'Seems like a bit of a shotgun wedding if you ask me,' said Glen, 'They've only known each other a few months.'

'Maybe she's pregnant,' said George moodily as thoughts of Roisin came to mind.

They settled down to watch the film.

Chapter Twenty-Four

George parked his car in the car park and they stepped out. Both wore smart suits and bow ties.

'I feel a bit like a fish out of water,' said Glen. 'Can't remember the last time I wore a suit.'

'What? Not even at work?'

'No, we can wear what we want at work.'

There were many people standing in groups around the church yard.

'Do you know any of these people?' asked George, feeling a bit lost among the unfamiliar faces.

'No. I only met Matt through my builder friend Roger, but Roger's gone to Australia for six months on a contract job so he won't be here. Some of the other builders that were working on the house might be here.'

'Lisa might think twice about marrying Matt when she sees you today,' quipped George.

'Give it a rest.'

'No, it's true, you missed out. It could've been you marrying her today. When you spurned her advances she fell for Matt on the rebound.'

'Did Roisin leave some romantic novels lying about the house when she left? Didn't know you were into Mills and Boon.'

George didn't respond. His thoughts turned to Roisin. He'd seen her the night before when she collected Robbie for the weekend and they'd hardly said two words to each other. He still found it hard to believe how they could go from being so much in love to being at the opposite side in court proceedings. Divorce. It was such a harsh word and something he'd felt strangely immune to; he'd believed that— like a deadly disease—it was something that happened to other people.

'Sorry, George. Shouldn't have mentioned her. You should try and forget her. You might meet a nice girl at the reception.'

'I'm not interested in finding someone here.'

'Me neither. Women always let you down in the end.'

'Yeah, well, keep that to yourself today. Matt obviously still believes in all that true love nonsense.'

Glen chuckled. 'We're a right pair of old saddos, aren't we? Who'd have thought a couple of good-looking blokes like us would end up alone?'

'You didn't have to be alone. Lisa would have chosen you over Matt any day.'

'Stop taking the piss. She's getting married, so let's change the record, please.'

'It's true, though. I bet she still has a thing for you.'

Glen stopped walking and folded his arms. 'How can I put this simply? You wouldn't know this, but when you're as attractive as I am, lots of women fall for you; the trick is not to waste your time with the phonies.'

'Um... I have broken a few hearts, I'll have you know.'

'When we're out together, it's me that the girls fancy. Face it.'

'Yeah, but when they start talking to us they change their minds.'

'Great. So bang goes your theory about Lisa fancying me, then. She probably wishes she was marrying you.'

'Keep your voice down,' whispered George, 'these people are her friends and family.'

They entered the church, which was already quite full of people.

'Wow, they have a lot of guests,' said Glen.

'Yeah, maybe you'll find love here.'

'Why are you on my case? Why aren't you looking for

love? Roisin's left you.'

'It's different for me. I have a son to think about. You're still hung up on a woman who left you years ago, so don't start on me.'

George thought of Belinda, his new nanny. He'd taken her on when Roisin left home, as he needed someone to look after Robbie while he was at work. It was an instant attraction for him. He'd found himself telling her that Rex had left the sale proceeds from the house to him and Glen, and they'd stayed up late into the night thinking of fun ways he could spend the money. The inevitable happened when he'd had a bit too much to drink and Belinda asked about Roisin: he'd become emotional when telling her about how she'd left him; Belinda offered a shoulder to cry on, and they ended up sleeping together. Although he'd expected her to say that it had been a mistake the next morning, she didn't. They'd continued to share a passionate romance. He hadn't told Glen and was still at the stage where he didn't believe it would last, so decided to keep it to himself.

'Wow, George, I wouldn't have invited you here if I knew you'd be so annoying,' boomed Glen. 'Can we just enjoy the ceremony? We'll have no end of women falling at our feet when we get the money from the sale of the old geezer's property.'

'When will we get the money? Do you know yet?' For some reason George thought again of Belinda as he said this, and pondered—as he had done quite frequently—whether she had only fallen for him because she knew he was coming in to money. He felt quite old compared to her and hated to think he'd end up a fool being snared by a young girl for his cash. He did think he was lucky to have found her, though; she had brought a bit of happiness into his life.

'I was meaning to tell you about that,' said Glen, interrupting his train of thought. 'It's going to take a bit longer than anticipated. That investor pulled out at the last minute. He heard stories about the history of the house and it put him off. I bet it was that blasted Lisa. The house is back on the market and the probate solicitor is keeping me updated. He says there's some interest.'

'I wondered why it was taking so long,' said George.

'I'll just be glad when it's sold; I've found a house in the south of France that I'm interested in.'

'Cool. A holiday home?'

'No, I'm thinking of moving out there permanently. A mate of mine lives over there; he married a French bird. Says it's great over there.'

'I don't like the sound of that. Who will I go to the pub with?'

'You'll have Tom and Jess.'

'They don't want to know me.'

'It's me they hate mostly. You'll be fine. What will you do with your share?'

'I want to sell the house and move out, start afresh; nearer Robbie's school, maybe—the houses there are nice but expensive.'

'Sounds good. You and Robbie are welcome to visit me in France.'

'Thanks.'

The wedding was pleasant. The evening reception led to dancing in open fields outside the hotel that had been booked as a venue.

At 12.15 a.m. the bride and groom said their goodbyes as they walked along shaking hands with the guests.

Glen noticed something dark on Matt's arm as he came closer to them. As Matt reached out his arm, Glen saw it clearly: a tattoo.

'Hey, Matt, I didn't know you had a tat; let's see. When did ya get it?' He pulled Matt's arms closer to him.

'While I was doing up the house,' said Matt. 'I kept having these whacky dreams.'

Glen took hold of his arm to see it more clearly. 'A sp-spider?' He dropped Matt's arm as if he'd been electrocuted.

'Yeah!' said Matt, cheerily. 'It's not a real one, you idiot!' He burst out laughing. 'You're scared of spiders?'

'No, I'm not.'

'Did you get it because of Rex?' asked George, transfixed, staring at the tattoo.

'Who's Rex?' asked Matt.

'The man who used to live at the house in Goldfern Road.'

'No. I got it because... Well, I'd wanted a tattoo for ages, but couldn't decide what to get. When I was working at the house at Goldfern Road, I kept dreaming of spiders.' He chuckled. 'Then my friend said he was having a tattoo done and asked if I wanted to go along, so I went with him. I wasn't planning to get one. I only went along to keep him company, but when I saw the artist's designs, this spider caught my eye. I thought it looked so cool. Lisa hates it.'

'The man who lived at the house you were working on used to dress up as a spider,' said George.

Matt's eyes widened. 'Wow. I didn't know that. You're pulling my leg, right?' He let out a nervous laugh.

'No,' said George, looking him in the eye.

Matt turned away.

Lisa appeared, having previously been chatting with another group of guests. 'C'mon, we've got to go,' she said to Matt. 'Oh, hi, Glen... and George, isn't it?' She flicked back her hair and fluttered her eyelashes at Glen.

'Hi,' said Glen and George in unison.

'I've been showing them my tat.'

'It's revolting. I nearly didn't marry him because of it. Brought back so many bad memories.' She leaned in and whispered to Glen, 'I never told Matt about Rex.'

'He knows now,' said George who was within earshot.

Lisa stared at George.

'What?' asked Matt.

'About the spider-man who used to live at eight Goldfern Road,' said George.

'A happy coincidence,' said Matt, smiling. He kissed Lisa and they said goodbye.

Chapter Twenty-Five

'We've had another offer on the house,' came Glen's voice over the phone.

'Wh-what time is it?' said George sitting up in bed.

'Nine o'clock.'

'It's Saturday. Couldn't you have waited to call me later?'

'No, because I wanted to get your opinion. The agent needs to know if we'll accept.'

'The agent? Isn't the solicitor dealing with them?'

'Yeah, but they don't work on Saturdays, so the agent called me. I asked the solicitor for the agent's details the other week so I could be kept in the loop. I got chatting to Joe, the agent, and he's a really nice guy. He promised to let me know about any offers.'

'So what's this offer?'

'It's a couple and they're relocating from out of town. They've offered two hundred thousand under the asking price.'

'So, eight hundred thousand?'

'Seven hundred and fifty thousand.'

'Maybe we should accept it—considering the history of the house.'

'I thought that. I mean, I'm sick of my job. The longer we wait for a buyer, the more time I'm stuck here. I need to move quickly if I'm gonna secure that house I want in France. So, if you agree, I'll let the agent know.'

'Yeah, that's fine,' said George.

'Cool. Apparently this couple don't have a property to sell, so we can get a quick sale.'

'Great.'

'Meet you there later?'

'Um...'

'C'mon; might be the last time we get to see it.'

'All right, about one o'clock?'

'See you there.'

Roisin and Hugh had stayed overnight with her parents after collecting Robbie from George that Friday night.

On Saturday afternoon, they left Robbie with Roisin's sister and went to view the house they were planning to purchase.

'I'm so excited! We'll finally be buying our own place together. It's close to Robbie's school as well, so I'll ask George if I can have Robbie during the week. It would make more sense. George works during the week, so he can have him at weekends.'

'The agent says that the seller wants a quick sale, as he's moving abroad,' said Hugh.

Roisin squeezed his hand as they arrived at the gate to the house. 'I feel like it's luck, you know? Right place, right time. This property was meant to be ours.' She grinned at Hugh and he kissed her forehead.

'I think you're right,' he said, as he unlatched the gate.

'I don't care what you say, Glen, this house still freaks me out and I can't wait until we finally sell it. When that investor pulled out, I got this really bad feeling like no one would ever buy it and we'd be stuck with it. It's like this spider-man freak is still there in my head and he's tormenting me.'

'I'm sure this couple will buy it. They're from out of town, so I doubt they've heard the stories about Rex,' said Glen. 'Try to think positively. The agent said in a few weeks the sale will be through and we'll have all the cash in our banks. I'm so excited about moving to France.'

A creaking sound interrupted his speech.

George jumped. 'What was that noise?'

'Don't worry, the spider freak is dead, it's not him.' Glen laughed, but then there were footsteps.

'Did you leave the front door open?' asked George.

'I don't think so,' said Glen, peeking out through the kitchen door. 'Oh no.' Closing the door carefully, he put a finger to his mouth and whispered, 'Is Roisin looking for a new home with her fella?'

George frowned. 'Yes, she is. She phoned me after she moved in with Hugh and said they want to move back to London. The bank he works for has agreed to relocate him, and she wants me to sell my house as part of the divorce settlement. She's taking some of the money as a deposit for her new house. I told you that before, didn't I?'

'It makes sense. The couple who are buying this place, they're from Surrey. Roisin and her new bloke live there, don't they?'

'Yeah, so what?'

'She's just gone into the living room. The agent must've given them a key.'

'Th-they're in the house? They... They want to buy this house?'

'Yeah.'

Pushing Glen out of the way, George opened the kitchen door and strode into the hallway.

'Wait!' called Glen.

George stopped at the entrance to the living room.

Glen ran up behind him.

Standing by the fireplace were Roisin and Hugh, staring at George.

'G-George? Wh-what're you doing here?' asked Roisin

eventually.

'I could ask you the same thing.' He folded his arms.

'Hugh and I have put an offer in on this place. Don't tell me you have, too?' Roisin raised her eyebrows. 'Have you been stalking me?'

'Fuck off,' said George.

Hugh stepped forward. 'Don't talk to her like that.'

'She's my wife and I'll talk to her however I want, you twat.'

Glen walked into the room and stood in front of George. 'There's been a misunderstanding,' he said. 'George and I are selling this place. The agent says a couple put an offer in this morning; I'm guessing that's you?'

'George?' Roisin glared at him, awaiting a response.

Hugh interjected, 'If this belongs to him, you have a right to claim a share in the divorce, surely? We need to talk to your lawyer about it.'

'I had no idea you owned this. You never told me you had another property,' Roisin barked.

'I don't own it, I just inherited the place—well, the proceeds of sale.'

'I'm going to have to speak to my lawyer about it.'

Just then, three shiny black circles sprouted on her forehead.

George's eyes widened. 'Look!' he said to Glen, pointing at her.

Glen leaned towards Roisin. 'What's that on your face?'

'What?' she said, as another two black marks appeared on her cheeks.

She glanced at Hugh and said, 'What're those black things on your face? I feel dizzy. Everything's blurry, like I've got double vision.'

He peered into the mirror above the fireplace as more

black circles developed on his forehead.

The couple looked at Glen and George as if expecting an explanation.

'Wh-what's happening?' said Glen.

'It's like my dream, and like the other time we were here and I thought you'd turned into a spider.'

Roisin screamed, 'Help!' She then shrank at an astonishing rate, as did Hugh. They had transformed into two black spiders, each one as big as a hand.

'Whoa, George, this is weird. Do you think there was anything in that beer we drank?'

'Th-this is exactly what happened the last time... I thought you'd turned into a spider... It's him, Glen.' George grabbed his friend's arm. 'It's The Spider. It's a game to him. This is all a trick. In a minute, Roisin and Hugh will come down the stairs or along the hallway. Stay calm.'

They both stepped back and watched the two arachnids crawling along the floor towards them.

'We should leave,' said Glen.

'We... We can't leave them here.'

'They're coming for us. What if they're poisonous or something?'

'Last time Theo stamped on the spider and then you came back; maybe that's what we have to do. You stamp on that one and I'll do this one.'

'*I've got you in my web, you'll never win,*' came a familiar voice.

'Did you hear—' asked George, looking at Glen, anxiety in his eyes.

'Y-yeah, it sounded like... Rex.'

George sighed with relief. 'Now do you believe me?'

'Shit. This is... fucked up.' Glen took two steps backwards.

'Wait, Glen! We have to kill them. Rex is behind this.'

159

He ran over to the spider that had been Hugh, and stomped on it.

'What have you done?'

'Kill the other one, Glen! Do it! Now!'

Glen ran over to the spider and stamped on it.

George covered his eyes.

The floor was now covered in blood. Deep red blood. Hundreds of little spiders bubbled out of the crimson fluid.

'What's happening?' screamed George.

'Quick, run!'

Glen tugged at his friend's arm and they ran out of the front door, slamming it shut behind them.

'What's going on?' said Glen, panting. 'Tell me this is some sort of bad dream...'

'We can't leave them.' George held his head. 'What if we've killed them?'

'It wasn't us! They turned into spiders, for fuck's sake!'

'I'm going back in,' said George. 'Please come with me. Please.' His eyes were brimming with tears.

'The house is possessed by that weirdo spider-man freak. If we go back in there we might not come out alive,' said Glen.

'It must've been some kind of illusion. It's Rex having fun at our expense. I need to go back in and make sure they're all right. Chances are they'll be in there chatting.'

'What? Did you see all those spiders?' Glen took a few steps backwards.

George fumbled for the key in his pocket and opened the front door. 'Those spiders couldn't have been real,' he said. 'If they were they'd be all over the house by now. There's no sign of them in the hallway.'

Glen followed him and they tiptoed slowly as if trying not to disturb whatever was in the house.

At the entrance to the living room, George stopped

and placed a hand over his mouth. 'Oh, my God. No... NO! NO!' He ran into the room.

Glen followed. 'Wh-what is it.'

George sat on the floor beside the fireplace staring at Roisin, who lay there covered in blood. Her body was twisted and bruised, giving the impression that she'd been trampled on by a large animal. Covering his face with his hands, he began to cry.

'We've killed them,' said Glen looking at the two prone bodies, bruised and torn.

'We killed them,' echoed George.

They heard gruff laughter in the room.

'The Spider always catches its prey. You're in my web. You lose.'

George and Glen ran out of the house and to George's car that was parked across the road.

'We have to get away from here fast,' Glen's voice dripped anxiety.

George slid into the driver's seat. 'Wait, Glen! We can't just run away.'

'We have to! As soon as they find the bodies, we'll be the number-one suspects.' Glen buckled his seatbelt. 'Quick, start the car.'

'Wait! Look!' George pointed to a couple walking up the street towards the house. Hugh and Roisin.

The two were smiling as if they didn't have a care in the world.

Hugh kissed Roisin on the forehead and opened the gate to 8 Goldfern Road.

Glen stared open-mouthed. 'It's them... But how?'

'They're alive. Stay down so they don't see us. We must have somehow been tricked by Rex. I told you it wasn't real.' George turned to Glen, relief clear in his wide eyes.

'Yeah, you were so sure it was an illusion you were bawling your eyes out a few moments ago.'

'I thought they were dead, I thought we'd killed them! How did you expect me to react?'

'I dunno. I'm sick of this. Let's hope they sign the contract quick, so we'll be free of this spider freak.'

'No,' said George. 'We can't sell to them.'

'Why? It's perfect.'

'For one, as soon as Roisin finds out I own half of it she'll pull out; didn't you hear what they said in there?'

'It wasn't really them.'

'I know but——'

'The contracts are in the executors' names, remember?' said Glen, 'She'll never know that you own the property.'

'I can't agree to sell to them.'

'Stop being so petty.'

'I'm not.' He looked at Glen, red-faced. 'If they buy the house, Robbie will be staying there at weekends or maybe even during the week. The house is haunted by a ghost who thinks it's funny to pretend to kill people. I don't want any link to the house and I don't want my son living there.'

'Fair enough, but what do we do then?'

'We tell the executors that we can't sell to them for personal reasons. We even ask them to take it off the market if we have to.'

'That would leave the property unsold. What about our money?'

'We should tell the solicitor we don't want the money.'

'What?'

'Think about it, Glen. It's brought us nothing but trouble; what if the money we get from it is cursed too?'

'I was looking forward to buying my house in France,' said Glen glumly.

'Yeah, but what if part of the deal is that the spider freak will follow us wherever the money goes. He could follow you to France.'

'That's ridiculous.'

'As ridiculous as watching two grown adults turn into spiders and then corpses in the space of ten minutes on a Saturday afternoon?'

'Hmm... You have a point.'

'Let's face it, this house and any money is cursed, and we're better off without it.'

Chapter Twenty-Six

Glen called the solicitor on Monday morning from his flat. George sat next to him on the sofa.

'Yes, we've decided—after a lot of thought—that we don't want the sale proceeds...' he said grumpily. 'Yes, I know it's unusual...' He looked skyward. 'Yeah, but the costs of the renovation can be taken from the sale, though, can't they?' He held his head as he listened. 'Yeah, we'll sign whatever you want.'

He pressed "end call" and looked at George again, his mouth in a sulk.

'So, can it be done?' asked George impatiently.

'Yeah, although I didn't understand the legal jargon—something about a disclaimer or renouncing. We have to sign something. He said it was unusual circumstances because we've renovated the house.'

'I heard you say something about the costs,' said George frowning. 'Your builder friends need to be paid.'

'He thinks they can be paid from the sale proceeds.'

'*Thinks?*'

'He's going to look into it. He said he's sure he can find a way round it.'

'How much did the builders want for the work?'

'A hundred grand.'

'Bloody hell. We can't afford that.'

'Stop panicking. It wouldn't make sense for the money not to be paid from the estate, would it?'

George exhaled loudly. 'I hope you're right.'

'I hope we're doing the right thing, letting the house go.'

'We are,' said George nodding wearily. 'I wish we'd turned it down before we went to the bother of doing it up.'

164

'One week, and the house will be ours!'

Hugh hugged Roisin.

'Wow! I'm so excited,' she said. 'I promise I'll pay you back when the money comes through from the sale of my old house. George is having trouble selling it. If you ask me, he's not putting much of an effort into it.'

'Who cares?' said Hugh, taking a bottle of champagne from the fridge. 'Now that contracts have been exchanged, I think we can celebrate.'

'I'll ask George tomorrow about having Robbie to live with us during the week. I miss him so much, and hate only being able to see him at the weekend.'

'Fine, whatever you want,' he said, touching her tummy. 'But remember, looking after a baby as well as Robbie will be hard work.'

'Robbie's at school most of the time. It'll be fine. Besides, he's looking forward to meeting his little sister.'

Roisin walked up the path to the house she used to share with George. Nostalgia and melancholia merged in her mind as she neared the door. They'd chosen the house together and were so happy when they first moved in. It was supposed to be the house they grew old in as a couple. It made her cynical about her imminent house move: she fully intended to grow old in that house with Hugh, but who knew what life had in store? Pushing the negative thoughts away, she rang the doorbell.

A woman opened the door. A pretty girl, in her twenties maybe. Long black hair and dark brown eyes. She smiled brightly at Roisin. 'Can I help you?'

Sensing an inexplicable twinge of jealousy, Roisin asked, 'Who are you?'

'I'm Mr Barnaby's nanny, Belinda. You must be Roisin.'

'Yes, I am.' Roisin entered the house and walked into the front room. 'Where's George?'

'He's on his way home. I've just put Robbie to bed.'

Roisin felt a twist of envy. This woman had put her son to bed. She missed Robbie and couldn't bear the thought of another woman looking after him. She fought the urge to go upstairs and take him away; instead she sat on the sofa.

'Will you be waiting for Mr Barnaby?' asked Belinda.

'Yes,' said Roisin, avoiding eye contact with the girl.

'In that case, is it all right if I leave? I usually work until seven, but he's late today, so—'

'Yes, yes, that's fine.'

She listened as the nanny put on her shoes and collected her bag from the kitchen. Eventually, she heard the door close as the girl left the house.

George opened the front door and walked in to find Roisin sitting on the sofa.

He recalled the horrors of Saturday afternoon and had to catch his breath.

'I didn't know you had a nanny,' said Roisin, without even saying hello.

'Wh-what?'

'Belinda. She was here when I came.'

'Belinda is a friend of a friend. I can't be at work and look after Robbie at the same time.'

Roisin stood up, 'I that case, you'll be glad to hear that you don't have to.'

He frowned. 'What?'

'Hugh and I have bought a house, not too far from

here. We've exchanged contracts. It'll be ours in a week's time. I want to take Robbie during the week and you can have him at the weekends.'

Goldfern Road? George thought, as panic set in.

'Oh, and by the way.' She flicked her hair back over her shoulder, 'Have you found a buyer for this place yet? I want my share. It's not fair on Hugh to have to pay the whole amount.'

'Where are you moving to?'

'Goldfern Road. It's a lovely house. Newly renovated. It's beautifully decorated; very modern.' She sauntered past him, 'By the way, I'm not happy about you employing a childminder for my son without my permission, and I'll be informing my solicitor about that. In future, any decisions about Robbie's welfare have to be agreed between us, okay?' She walked towards the front door.

'I won't let Robbie stay with you in that house.'

'Why not?' She spun around then exhaled deeply. 'You're jealous of me and Hugh, aren't you?'

'No.'

'You have to move on. I'm having a baby with Hugh and we're very happy together. Why can't you be happy for me?'

'Get out, Roisin.'

'Don't worry, I'm leaving. You'll be hearing from my solicitor.'

When she slammed the door behind her, George waited for the voice, expecting *The Spider* to say he'd caught him in a web—but there was only silence.

'We've got to do something, Glen! They're buying Rex's house,' shouted George into his phone.

'Slow down, mate. Who's buying it?'

'Roisin and Hugh. They've signed the contracts. They're moving in soon.'

'The spider freak might leave them alone. They didn't have anything to do with—'

'They did, they're my family.'

'No, not anymore. Even the spider freak knows that. You're getting divorced.'

'But Robbie's my son; if he wants revenge he might hurt him.'

'Meet me in the pub and we'll talk about it. I need to drown my sorrows; been feeling like crap this week. The house I wanted in France has been sold. I'm stuck here in this dingy flat.'

'That money was cursed.'

'Yeah, well, looks like we ain't seen the last of Mr Spider if your wife's bought the property.'

'Don't say that.'

'See you later.'

'I can't come to the pub, I have to look after Robbie. You come here.'

Half an hour later, Glen sat in George's living room drinking whisky.

'So what are we gonna do, Glen? I have to stop the sale. Any ideas?'

'You can't stop the sale.'

'We must be able to do something.'

'What? Burn the house down?' said Glen, swigging his whisky.

George recalled the flames billowing from the house when he'd set it alight. He walked over to the window.

'Sorry, mate,' said Glen. 'I wasn't having a dig. It just

came out.'

'It's okay.' George tried his best to block the terrifying scenes from his mind. 'Would you be willing to do it?' he asked, desperation fuelling his question.

Glen blinked exaggeratedly. 'You've got to be kidding, right? And, why me?'

'Because... I dunno, because you're better at that sort of thing than I am,' said George, pacing the living room. 'Things don't get to you. I've been a nervous wreck since that spider-man captured us, but you...'

'You make me sound like I haven't got a conscience. I do still get stressed when I think back to it, you know. I don't like to dwell on it.'

'You're better at leaving stuff behind. I'd love to leave all of this behind, but every time I think we're rid of him, he strikes back.'

'Strikes back? You're talking like he's still alive.'

'He's still out there... You saw it yourself. Look, Glen, I think burning the place down might be the only option we have.'

'Y-you're going to burn it down again?'

George sat next to him. 'No, I thought maybe you could.'

'No way. You're the one who got us into this mess, you can get us out.'

'You have a selective memory. There were a couple of times you nearly killed Rex, smashing bricks over his head when we were trying to get out of the house. And you shot those thugs and Rex with that weird gun when we were escaping. Remember?'

'That was different, it was self-defence. I didn't go back into the house deliberately to kill him.'

'So, it's all my fault?'

'No, but... if he wasn't dead he wouldn't be seeking

revenge from the grave, would he?'

'He was as dangerous when he was alive.'

'I'm not setting fire to the house, mate, forget it. I'm too good-looking to end up in prison; can you imagine what would happen to me in there?'

'Be serious. We have to do something: my son's life is at risk. You're the one who convinced me to go into the house in the first place.'

'Er... you're the one who told me about the house. I wouldn't have even known it existed if you didn't tell me.'

George held his head. 'Oh this isn't getting us anywhere.'

'Look, your main concern is Robbie living in the house, right? All you have to do is refuse to let Roisin have him. Leave London. Take him somewhere she can't find you.'

'Kidnap my own child?'

'It's not kidnapping if you're the parent, is it?'

'It is. I'd probably get arrested.'

'You can prove she's an unfit mother and refuse to allow her to have contact.'

'I couldn't stop her seeing Robbie.'

'She had an affair. She left Robbie alone in the house so she could carry on an affair with the neighbour. You don't have to stop her seeing him, just not let her have sleepovers, then Robbie won't be staying at the house and old Rex can't get to him.'

George stared at Glen. The walls were closing in on him, options running out. Although they'd escaped the dark basement and the chains that had held them there, George's fear was as real as it was back then.

'You're scaring me, George; why are you staring?'

Glen's voice shook him out of his introspection. 'I can't see a way out of this. I don't know how everything got so complicated.'

'It was The Spider—'

'The spider,' said George, standing up quickly.

'Yes, Rex.'

'No.' George's mind went back to the night when Robbie asked him to kill a spider in his bedroom. He recalled how he'd felt guilty for a moment but then forgot that as soon as he tucked Robbie into bed. 'What if this all started because I killed a spider,' he said.

Glen raised an eyebrow and poured another glass of whisky. 'You're not making any sense.'

George sat down again. 'Not long before we went to the house, I killed a spider in Robbie's bedroom.'

'Um... you mean that was the first spider you ever killed?'

'No. No, of course not... But... the spider might've been some kind of, I dunno, supernatural spider.'

'If it was, you wouldn't have been able to kill it. And what does a spider in your house have to do with that freak? He'd been planning his murders long before you killed the spider. And, I've killed about a hundred spiders in my lifetime.'

'Maybe they're taking revenge.'

'What?'

'It's something Robbie said when I killed that spider for him. He said that because I'd killed it, the spider's friends would be coming to kill us.'

'He's a four-year-old. Kids have wild imaginations.'

'I know, but—'

'You need a drink.' He refilled George's glass.

George stared at the amber liquid blankly, his mind fuzzy with conflicting thoughts. 'I'm not sure how we can ever be free. We may as well still be in that basement. He's trapped us.'

'Do what I said. Stop Roisin having Robbie to stay over

at the house.'

'It won't work.' George got to his feet. 'I have to burn it down.'

'You're not thinking straight. It's too risky; you could get caught. And, it's dangerous. Besides, it'll only delay matters. They'll claim on the buildings insurance, and once it's been fixed they'll move in anyway.'

George placed his hands over his face in frustration.

'I'm sure you're getting wound up over nothing.'

'No! Rex is doing all of this. He's the one who made Roisin have an affair with Hugh, and he's the one who made them purchase the house. He said we're in his web, didn't he?' George tried to shut out the memory of Rex's voice but, try as he might, the words "You're in my web" repeated in his head a few times; echoes of the words he dreaded to hear. It took momentous effort to shut it out.

'How can he do anything? He's dead.'

Glen's voice gave welcome relief from the torment in his mind. 'You saw what he did at the house,' said George, over the voice still playing on repeat in his head.

'An illusion. We could've been drunk or imagined it.'

'What? Both of us, at the same time?'

Glen shrugged. 'There's this phenomenon called "multiple effect", or something; I read about it.'

'You're a mine of useless information. Did you read about it in the same paper as the one about spontaneous combustion?'

'Ha, ha! That's a real phenomenon, you know. You're just reading the wrong stuff—like Mills and Boon, for example.'

'Okay, then. What's "multiple effect"?'

'It's like when two people make the same discovery at the same time. Did you know that the jet engine was invented by three different people at the same time and they didn't know each other?'

'What's that got to do with Rex?'

'It means that the mind can read other people's minds. Something to do with brainwaves. I don't understand the science behind it.'

'I've heard a theory that there are all these ideas out there just floating around in space somewhere, and inventors or creators sometimes hit upon the same one at the same time.'

'Hmm... anything's possible, I suppose. But isn't it more likely that we kind of picked up on each other's brainwaves that day at the house?'

'What like telepathy? So I imagined them turning into spiders, maybe because of what had happened before—you know, with you turning into a spider—'

'I didn't turn into a spider.'

'You did. I saw you. Anyway, are you saying that you picked up on me imagining them turning into spiders and then you imagined it too?' George wrinkled his nose. 'Sounds a bit far-fetched.'

'As far-fetched as what actually happened?'

George looked into Glen's eyes.

'Stop staring at me like that, I keep thinking you're a zombie.'

George shook his head. 'He threatened me. I was alone in my kitchen and I heard his voice; he said that he'd possess my second child and continue his mission.'

'Problem solved then. Don't have any more children. He obviously needs a body to possess. Besides, I think it was all hot air; he never had power to do anything, even in life. He was only a bitter man who felt insecure in himself and wanted to take out his sense of failure on everyone else. I think he was trying to scare us.'

'He's never gonna go away though, is he? He'll always

be there threatening and causing problems.' George held his head.

'Exorcism, that's what we need. We'll get a priest round to get rid of him.'

'D'you believe in all that mumbo jumbo?'

'I didn't believe in ghosts until last weekend,' said Glen. 'Can't hurt to try it.'

Chapter Twenty-Seven

George met Glen in the pub at lunchtime on Saturday.

'You're looking perky,' said Glen as he greeted him.

'Maybe that's because we might have finally got rid of Rex.'

Glen raised an eyebrow. 'Tell me more. No, wait, get me a beer and then tell me more.'

George rolled his eyes and went to the bar.

'So,' said Glen, sipping his beer after George's return, 'did you go for the exorcism in the end, then?'

'No. Didn't have to. Roisin bumped into Lisa when they were moving in and she told her all about Rex and how he'd died there. They've put the house back on the market and she's staying with her mum.'

'Wow. Blabbermouth Lisa actually did something worthwhile for a change. I bet she was the one who put all the other potential buyers off. Bitch.'

'She probably wanted you to live there.'

'Still playing that broken record, George? She's happily married now, remember?'

'She's bitter about you spurning her advances. She married Matt on the rebound; she most likely regrets it now.'

'Huh! I see you're still reading those romance novels.'

'It wouldn't hurt *you* to read more fiction. Apparently, it makes you more empathetic.'

'Why would I want to be pathetic?'

'Empath— Oh, never mind. Look, so we missed out on the money from the house sale. We should thank Lisa; she did us a favour. I still reckon it would have been cursed. We're better off without it.'

'I'm cursed regardless, having to live here instead of

my dream house,' complained Glen.

'Look on the bright side: I haven't had any nightmares for a whole week, and there's no sign of Rex anywhere. I think he got bored of chasing us, or finally passed over to the other side, whatever happens with dead people.'

'Great news. We can go back to some normality at last. I was sick of staring at your miserable face.'

'Yeah, well, let's hope it's the end of it.'

'Wait! So if Lisa told Roisin about Rex dying, does she know we were there?'

'No. Roisin didn't seem to know anything about that. I was holding my breath when she mentioned it, but she just said she'd found out that a serial killer had been living in the house and died there. She didn't want to have anything to do with it. It freaked her out. She said that she was worried in case there was anyone who knew him and would want to retaliate by targeting the house... She also said she was worried it might be haunted. She sounded a bit paranoid, to be honest, but I was just glad she didn't mention anything about me being involved. I had a flashback to when we saw her turning into a spider, you know, when she was threatening to go to her solicitor and claim part of the house. Can you imagine if she found out? I wouldn't put it past her to try and claim something even now.'

'But she can't now we don't own it, can she?'

'Yeah, she might try to get compensation or something.'

'You worry too much. The house is nothing to do with us anymore.'

'I'd just prefer if she knew nothing about what we did. I can't wait until she sells, then we can forget about it for ever.'

'Yeah well, at least you know they won't be living there; there's no risk of Rex getting to Robbie.'

'Yeah, I hated the idea of Robbie living there.'

'Looks like we can put the freaky spider-man behind us, at last.'

George nodded.

Glen raised his beer glass. 'Here's a toast to the demise of The Spider, long may he rot in Hell.'

'I'll drink to that.' George chuckled.

'Don't look round, but guess who's just walked in.'

'You look worried. Who is it?' George stiffened.

'Oh my God, you didn't think? Don't be stupid. Rex is dead. It's not him.'

George's shoulders relaxed.

'Don't bite my head off, but I really think you need to get some counselling.'

'I don't. I'm fine. It was only because we were talking about him when you said someone had come in. I got a shiver down my back, you know, like when we were children and we used to say someone had walked over your grave.'

'Oh yeah, I remember that.'

'So who came in?'

'Tom-Tom and Jess,' said Glen.

'We should start talking to them again.'

'They're the ones who stopped talking to us. Let *them* apologise.'

Tom and Jess approached them.

George felt awkward being so estranged from these people who had been his friends for as long as he could remember. Their friendship had been another casualty in the war against Rex. The thought filled him with a determination to make amends.

'Can we sit here?' asked Tom.

'It's a free country,' said Glen.

'Ah, Tom, Jess, how are you? We've missed our chats,

haven't we, Glen?' gushed George.

Glen looked at him sideways. 'Did the barmaid slip something into your drink when you weren't looking?'

'Ignore him.' George waved a hand and gestured for the couple to join them. 'Sit down, sit down.'

Jess and Tom sat together opposite them.

'We wanted to say that we're sorry for what happened,' said Tom. 'We were out of order. That money is yours, fair and square; after all, we were too scared to go into the house. You deserve it. We were being childish, and we want to apologise.'

'No need to apologise. We were not exactly ourselves. The trauma of being in the house changed us a bit.'

'Speak for yourself,' said Glen.

A brief awkward silence followed, then Tom said, 'We have some great news to share. First, let me go and get some drinks in. What would you like?'

'Another beer would be nice,' said Glen.

'Um... yeah, the same,' said George.

Jess smiled at Tom. 'Just an orange juice for me.'

Tom left to get the drinks.

Jess excused herself to go to the toilet.

Glen waited until the couple were out of earshot, then whispered to George, 'I can see what's happening here, mate.'

'What?'

'She's having an orange juice—no alcohol; they have "great news" to share. She's pregnant. And what's more, they only want to get chummy with us because they still think we've got money and they think that because they're expecting a baby we'll suddenly offer them handouts. They've always been the same, them two. I say we nip it in the bud.'

'I dunno, Glen. We've been friends with them since

uni. Maybe, if she is pregnant, they just want to share the news with us.'

'You're too much of a soft touch.'

Tom returned with the drinks. 'Where's Jess?'

'Toilet,' said George.

'Right.'

'So why the sudden change of heart?' said Glen.

'I suppose it's because of our news,' said Tom. 'I won't tell you until Jess gets back. Let's just say, it's changed our perspective a bit.'

Glen gave George a knowing look.

Jess returned.

'So will you tell them, or shall I?'

'You can,' said Jess, still smiling.

'We're pregnant,' announced Tom.

Jess grinned and took his hand.

'Great news,' said George.

'It is. We've wanted a child for a long time and we thought we'd never have one,' said Jess.

'Congratulations.' Glen raised his beer glass.

'We were talking about stuff the other day,' said Tom, 'and you two have been our closest friends for a long time; we felt bad about what happened. It changes your perspective when you're going to become a parent. I'm sure you know that already, George.'

George nodded.

'I suppose we knew you'd be happy for us.'

'Or is it because you need more money when you're bringing up a kid?'

'Glen—'

'No, George, I have to say this.' Glen turned his attention back to Tom. 'C'mon Tom-Tom, you two have been avoiding us like the plague for ages, how do you think we felt, huh?'

Jess left the table.

'You're upsetting Jess,' said Tom. 'You are so wrong, Glen. You don't know how wrong you are. We wanted to share this news with you because you are two of our oldest friends. I think we made the wrong decision. I'm sorry you can't find it in your heart—'

'Piss off, Tom-Tom, your wife needs you. Real friends don't disown their friends when they don't give them a bit of money. You are so embarrassing.'

'*Real* friends would give their friends money when they're in need. We were broke back then and you were loaded. Real friends help each other. That's why we were upset.'

'Look,' interjected George. 'Let's not fall out over this.'

'Huh! That happened a while ago. I'm just annoyed that I didn't see their true colours years ago,' groaned Glen.

'You couldn't just forgive and forget, could you?' said Tom. 'Have to hold a grudge. We were willing to let you back into our lives even after—'

'Er... We weren't the ones in the wrong,' stated Glen.

'I'm wasting my breath.' Tom stood up and went over to the bar where Jess was standing.

'Weren't you a bit harsh?' said George when Tom was out of earshot. 'They're expecting a baby; they must be stressed out.'

'The truth of the matter is, no matter how I feel, we can't help them, can we? We're as broke as they are.'

'I know, but—'

'No buts. They're not *real* friends.'

'We might have been the ones in the wrong back then. Think about it: we were getting carried away with having all that money. Tom's right, we've been friends with them since uni. Maybe we should have considered giving them some money.'

'It doesn't matter either way, because the money was never ours, and now we're in debt.'

'Debt?'

'Yeah, the builders want paying. I've managed to stall them for a bit, but they won't wait for ever. They want their hundred grand.'

'B-but I thought the money was coming out of the estate.'

'I told you, I asked the solicitor and he said something about having to look into it. We did the work on the house when we weren't the legal owners—'

'Yeah, but that was agreed with the executors.'

'Let me finish. He said that we've added value to the estate by doing the work, so he'll try to find a way round it.'

'Well, he's taking his time. I thought that would be done and dusted by now.'

'You worry too much. It'll be fine.'

'Let's just hope it's not another one of Rex's tricks.'

George looked over at Tom and Jess, thinking about how Rex had ruined so much of his life. It felt as if pieces of the existence he once knew were fragmenting and it was up to him to retrieve them and put them back together again. 'Glen, I'm going to go and chat with Tom and Jess; let them know there's no hard feelings.'

'Do what you want.'

Chapter Twenty-Eight

'Turns out Tom has a new job working at a bank and is earning loads of money.'

'When did you hear that?' asked Glen.

George sipped his beer. 'Last time we were in here when you had that argument.'

'It wasn't an argument.'

'Anyway, apparently they were being sincere about being sorry.'

'Hmm... maybe I was a bit hasty.'

'Just a bit.'

'So have you been having any more nightmares?'

'No.' George smiled and for the first time in a long while felt able to breathe freely again. 'I truly believe Rex has gone.'

'Brilliant. And the solicitor says they'll pay the builders from the house sale; so they're off our backs now, too. Looks like everything's working out for the best.'

'That's a relief. Oh, and I have some news: I have a new woman.' Thoughts of the passionate nights he'd shared with Belinda came to the forefront of his mind. He hadn't been able to stop thinking about her. Finally, his life seemed to be back on track.

'Oooh! How did you find time to find a woman?' spurted Glen, 'I'm the good-looking one.'

'Yeah, but you ignore all the women who fancy you.'

'Who? Lisa?'

'Not only Lisa; I can't count the times women have come on to you in this pub. You treat them like shit.'

'I don't.'

'You do.'

'Forget about that, I want to hear about your new

woman.'

George smiled again, wishing Belinda were here now. 'I didn't have to go out looking for her. She came to me. She's Robbie's nanny. Belinda. We've been seeing each other; I didn't want to say anything before, in case it didn't work out. I really like her, and Robbie loves her too.'

'Does that mean you'll be spending less time with me?'

'Probably. Sorry. But you need to get out there, start dating again. You can't keep mourning whats-her-name. Whenever you break up with your girlfriends you say it's because you should have married Petula.'

'Yeah, it's gonna be engraved on my gravestone: Here lies the best-looking bloke in the world—he should have married Petula.'

'Why are you so hung up on her?' George laughed. 'She wasn't all that. You could do so much better.'

'I'd like to see her again, now we're older. She understood me, y'know?'

'You're like a broken record.'

'It's better than having a broken marriage.'

'Everything happens for a reason. If I hadn't of broken up with Roisin, I may never have met Belinda. She's gorgeous.'

'Stop showing off.'

'I'm not.'

'Just remember that not long ago you were sure that Rex had cursed you and was out to ruin your life. What if Belinda is another pawn in his game?'

'Nothing you say can bring me down from my cloud, Glen. The Spider is in the past. I was going through some kind of post-traumatic stress, but now the nightmares are gone and I feel happy.'

'Good to hear it, mate.'

'Now we have to find you a girlfriend. Maybe Belinda

knows someone.'

Glen waved his hand to dismiss the idea. 'I've decided to look for Petula. Nowadays it's easy to do a Facebook search, isn't it?'

'Are you sure that's a good idea? Isn't it like moving backwards? There was a reason you two broke up; do you really want to go there? Besides, you have no idea what her life is like now.'

'I just think that there must be a reason I can't forget her, why it's never worked out with all the others.'

'She broke your heart. She can do it again.'

'I'm going to look for her. What have I got to lose?'

'I'm surprised you haven't looked for her before, to be honest.'

'I'd be lying if I said I didn't. I've searched her name online a few times over the years.'

'Stalker.'

'Yeah, well. I've never done anything about it. I usually chicken out.'

'What's changed?'

'Not sure. None of us are getting any younger, are we?'

'True. Let me know what happens.'

Chapter Twenty-Nine

Petula Harrigan wiped her nose on her sleeve and cursed the fact that they didn't provide tissues, then laughed at herself through a bitter sneer. Seven days in prison. *Better than paying the fine*, she thought. She'd somehow managed to avoid having much contact with the other inmates. Didn't think of herself as an inmate. It was the first time she'd gone to prison and she wasn't in any hurry to return. Today was release day. Nobody knew where she was. She'd told Ebony, her best friend, that she'd be spending a week in Cambridge catching up with an old friend. She'd amazed herself that she managed to keep the court hearing, solicitor appointments, and the police station interview, secret. No one knew, and no one could ever find out. Even the benefits office were unaware. Her signing-on day wasn't until next Wednesday.

Stealing electrical equipment—or attempting to steal it —things she didn't even need, to get out of financial trouble. She'd had no idea where she would have sold the iPads, just took the display models and fled, not knowing they were all hooked up to alarms. The noise the alarm made as she tried to leave the building, still rang in her ears, a niggling reminder of yet another way she had failed in life.

Usually she'd have been given a caution, "a slap on the wrist", as one of the inmates put it: Jessica Longfellow, a woman experienced in all things criminal. Studying a course in criminology while in prison, Jessica wanted to be a defence lawyer when she got out. She still had a few years of her manslaughter sentence to serve.

'It should've been a slap on the wrist,' she'd said snootily when Petula told her what she was in for. 'It's not as if it's a serious crime, is it? If you ask me, they send too many people like you to jail; it's so overcrowded in 'ere.'

Strangely, Petula felt slighted by the comment, kicking herself for not lying about her crime. She should have said she'd committed murder: that would've wiped the smirk off Jessica's face.

'I have a history,' she found herself saying. 'Have been found in possession of drugs before and also have a few previous shoplifting stints on my record.' Even as the words came out of her mouth, she knew it sounded lame, but she comforted herself with the thought that soon she'd be out in the real world while Jessie and her type rotted away inside.

Stepping out of Holloway Prison that drizzly Tuesday morning, Petula took a deep breath of polluted London air, and looked around at the old buildings in need of repair under grey clouds. She promised herself to clean up her act. *Living in this grotty city, that's what's done it. Sucked the life out of me.*

She took the bus to her flat, pleased she had remembered to top up her Oyster card before being locked up. On arriving at Peppercorn Mansions, she made her way up to the third floor using the staircase, wondering for the umpteenth time about the irony and perhaps sarcasm that went behind naming the place "Mansions": some rich developer having a laugh while he or she lived in a real mansion in an idyllic country setting.

She hated using the lift; it invariably smelt of urine and there were discarded condoms or hypodermic needles lying around too many times to mention.

The staircase wasn't much better, but at least there'd be less chance of being confined in a small space with a psycho. The first time she'd been tempted to take drugs was on meeting Colin in the lift not long after the housing association allocated the flat at Peppercorn Mansions to her. She'd been so happy to finally have a place of her own, and in those days the estate was quite respectable. Colin had been handsome. Tall, dark, and handsome. He'd been smoking a spliff and winked at her when she got into the lift. She'd fancied him straight away. He was dressed in a leather jacket, his hair slicked back with gel in a fashionable style: slightly long at the front and covering his ears. He resembled a model she'd seen in *Vogue* not too long before.

He looked smart and smelled of a sensuous aftershave.

Colin had offered her a spliff, and when she revealed that she'd only recently moved into the estate he asked her out for a drink that evening, by way of welcoming her to "The Peppercorn" as it was known locally. She'd agreed and went on to have a passionate three-month relationship with him. He was a criminal who dabbled in drug dealing and had access to all sorts of drugs. She soon became a regular drug user, experimenting with various addictive substances, and had taken to shoplifting to fund her habit. Ironically, Colin ended their relationship citing her excessive drug abuse as the reason he couldn't stand to be around her. It took her months to wean herself off the addiction.

She regretted meeting him, and hoped she'd never see him again. Thankfully, he'd now left The Peppercorn and, the last she'd heard, he was serving a ten-year sentence for armed robbery.

Arriving at the door of her flat, she promised herself she'd get a job and move out of London as soon as she could afford to. It was unbearable being cooped up in the flat. It wasn't far removed from the jail cell.

She prayed the electricity hadn't been cut off, couldn't remember if she'd paid the most recent bill. She wanted to go online and catch up with her best friend, Ebony, on Facebook. They were online friends; she'd never met Ebony, but she called her "best friend" because she didn't have any real friends.

She'd opened a Facebook account years ago, but only started using it recently. In the past couple of years, finding herself increasingly alone, she'd found solace in an online community.

After discovering she had quite an eye for photography, she'd bought herself an old camera from a charity shop and started to take pictures of the local area. She'd go on walks every morning and take photographs of the sky, trees, birds, flowers. She loved posting them to Facebook. It took a while to upload them, as her computer was old: her brother gave it to her years ago when he'd upgraded his own computer. She had no idea where her brother lived now. He'd moved to Scotland when he got married and they lost touch after he found out she was on drugs.

She'd tried to get in touch with him recently, sent a letter to his last known address but didn't hear back from him. She'd searched online to no avail; his name didn't show up in a Google search. It seemed almost as if he'd disappeared from the planet. Losing her only sibling made her feel all the more lonely. Both her parents were dead. They'd been in their forties when they started a family, so by the time Petula was at university they were already pensioners. Her mother had passed away ten years ago and her father never got over the death: he'd killed himself the year afterwards. They'd written Petula out of their wills when they found out she was taking drugs.

Meeting Ebony online served as a lifeline for Petula. They exchanged messages regularly. Unlike Petula, Ebony's life seemed idyllic, at least from an observer's point of view. Ebony was married with two beautiful daughters. She posted endless photographs on Facebook of her "princesses". Sometimes Petula felt jealous, but mostly, she was glad to have Ebony as a friend, even if she did live hundreds of miles away.

Petula pressed the power button on her computer, keeping her fingers crossed that it would turn on. Thankfully it did. It took over a minute to load. Then she clicked on the Internet icon and logged on to Facebook. Sure enough, a message was waiting for her. It gave her a warm feeling inside knowing someone somewhere cared for her.

Clicking on the little red notification, she frowned: the message wasn't from Ebony. It was from a man. About to ignore it—assuming it must be from one of those spammers who send random "hi u are so pretty" messages—something far away in her memory stirred when she read his name. *Glen.* She'd known a Glen at university. They'd had a fling. It'd lasted a few months and at the time she'd called him her "soulmate"—when she still believed in things like that. She'd ended the relationship, but couldn't remember why.

This man, who'd sent the message, called himself Glen R. She racked her brain trying to remember what her boyfriend's surname had been. Redman. Yes, it began with R. She decided to read the message.

Hi, I'm not sure if you are the same Petula I dated at Uni. While searching on the Internet, I came across your profile. There's no photo........ only that flower. It's a nice photo, but I can't see any photos of you because your account is private. I'm Glen Redman. If you're the Petula I dated at uni, please let me know. Would luv to see u again. Glen.

He'd attached a photograph of himself. Her heart fluttered at the thoughts that were evoked by the familiar face. He still looked handsome, in a rugged type of way, and she remembered how in love with him she'd been as a young girl.

She thought of all the times recently that she'd prayed for a way out of her current predicament. Could Glen be a way out? Would he be able to offer her a chance to be happy? It was all coming back to her now... flashbacks conjured from the image of this long-lost love. She'd ended their relationship after becoming involved with another man, a man she'd met on holiday in Spain. Martino had swept her off her feet with promises of lifelong love. She'd fallen for him in a big way. She hadn't had any contact with Glen for a few weeks, as they were on a break from university, and somehow she'd been taken in by Martino. Their love affair lasted for a few months, but when she returned to England it became a long-distance relationship and hard to maintain, even though she tried her best.

Martino ended up marrying a local girl a year later and even invited Petula to the wedding. She'd cried herself to sleep when she received the invitation, realising their relationship had meant nothing to him.

Hi Glen, yes, it's me Petula. I remember you. A tear came to her eye as she typed the words.

An instant reply came back: **That's so cool. Where do you live now? We should meet up!**

She looked at her dingy flat, and walked over to the mirror. Her clothes were ragged and she needed a haircut. He'd never recognise her like this. At university, she'd been so different. Confident. Young. Always wore the latest fashions. *I can't meet him.*

She didn't reply to the message. Best to let him remember her as the girl she used to be. A fantasy version of herself was better than the reality, and if she lived in Glen's mind as a fantasy, maybe on some level she'd be free of this life that had become so hard to endure.

She switched off the computer and laid down on her bed, trying to block out the broken reminders of the past.

Chapter Thirty

Glen waited but there was no reply.

He knew she'd been online a minute ago, now nothing. *She must be ignoring me*, he thought, then wondered whether she might have small children who'd distracted her away from the Internet, or perhaps her husband had called her from another room and they'd gone out together for a romantic afternoon in the park.

He thought about sending her a friend request, but then he would know for certain her relationship status. In his imagination he'd created a version of her who was single and, like himself, had been waiting for a reunion. He recalled how she used to call him her soulmate.

Shrugging, he pressed the 'Add Friend' link on her page and waited. Nothing. Two minutes passed... five minutes...

He busied himself by scrolling down the news feed, pictures of cats, quotes from the Dalai Lama and other well-known people—many of them long dead. Funny how in the modern world people revered those who'd died yet could post so much negative stuff about people who were still living. Glen mused that the thing to do to get any respect was to die. Preferably after leaving a few vague words of wisdom behind.

Glen waited but soon grew jaded. Still no notification about his friend request.

Feeling frustrated, he put down his phone and went into the kitchen to make some lunch.

At 6 p.m. Petula rose from her bed and sat on the edge of it. She felt hungry, so put on her slippers and padded to the kitchen. On opening the fridge door she remembered that she hadn't bought any food.

Her kitchen was invariably stocked with the bare minimum, as she lived from week to week using her benefits to pay for supplies. In the fridge, a small piece of cheese sat alone on one of the shelves, and some out-of-date milk taunted her from the compartment in the door. The tomatoes in the vegetable tray were shrivelled.

She looked in the cupboard and found a few slices of bread that must have been there for a couple of weeks. Mould sprouted from the crust and there were suspicious white patches on the slices.

She scraped off the obvious mould and placed the bread in the toaster, then sliced the cheese and chopped the only tomato that still looked edible. It was the best food she'd eaten for over a week. The prison food had made her want to retch.

Preparing a cup of tea without milk, Petula settled down in front of the TV to watch the news.

As images of war, and of refugees struggling to make their way to a safe haven flashed before her on the screen, it struck her that she was one of the lucky ones. Just having her freedom was amazing and she wanted to hold on to that feeling. She decided that tomorrow she would make an effort to find a job. Any job. A reason to get up in the morning. And she promised herself to clean up her act: no more drink, and no more drugs; no more wasting her money or her life. From now on, she'd be making something of herself.

Distantly, thoughts of Glen's invitation were hovering, but she put them to the back of her mind; she couldn't think of meeting up with him, not yet. When she had a job, when she did her hair, when she bought some new clothes. For now, it would serve to motivate her and keep her moving in the right direction.

Chapter Thirty-One

Glen and George met at George's house in the evening for a drink.

'What are all these boxes?' asked Glen, nodding at the large cardboard boxes lined up in the hallway.

'Didn't I tell you? I've found a buyer for this place. I have to sell so Roisin can get her share. I thought I'd get a head start with packing the stuff.'

'Right. Let me know if you need any help with it. Where are you gonna be staying?'

George led him into the living room, wanting to ignore the question. He'd been looking around for suitable rental properties in the area, but so far had failed to find anything within his budget. He feared Roisin would end up taking Robbie if he couldn't afford decent accommodation for himself and the boy. He couldn't bear the thought of Robbie living with Roisin and Hugh full time. The burden of the fear weighed down on him. 'I'll find somewhere,' he mumbled a half-hearted response to his friend.

'You can sleep on my sofa until you find something else.'

'Thanks,' said George, 'but I have to find a place suitable for Robbie to live.'

'Houses around here are expensive.'

'Don't you think I know that?' George blurted, a bit too forcefully. 'Sorry,' he mumbled.

'It must be stressful. All seems a bit unfair, if you ask me; she was the one who ran off and had an affair, surely you should get to keep this place, and Robbie.'

'She put—well, her parents put a large deposit down when we bought the house, so she wants it back.' George sat on the sofa.

'Sorry, mate.'

'It's for the best. Too many memories in this place.'

'True. Where's Belinda?' asked Glen. 'I was hoping to meet her.'

'She works in a pub three nights a week after she's finished with the baby-sitting here. Tonight's one of those nights.'

'Maybe she can get us free drinks.'

'The pub's not local, so it wouldn't be worth travelling there for the free drinks.'

'You're not trying to hide her from me, are you? She's not a minger, is she?'

'You're pathetic, Glen. All you think about is how women look. There's a lot more to relationships, you know.'

'So she *is* a minger.'

'No, she's very pretty actually, but that's got nothing to do with why I'm with her.'

'Yeah, right. Anyway, aren't you gonna offer me a drink?'

George had already set out two glasses and some beer cans on the coffee table.

Glen sat next to him on the sofa. 'Is Robbie with Roisin today?'

'No, he's upstairs.'

'Have they sold Rex's place yet?'

Unwanted thoughts descended. Snapshots in George's mind, reminders of what had happened. He could see the faces of the men he'd killed, their eyes accusing him. Anxiety took hold. Every time he remembered the house, the same dark memories disturbed him, making him uneasy. He shook away the black feeling. 'I don't think so, otherwise she'd be taking Robbie to live with her during the week. That's her plan, anyway. I'm not very happy about it.'

'Have you had any of those weird dreams lately?'

'No, thank God,' said George, once again on edge as if he might have spoken too soon. 'I think The Spider has well and truly left us.' He inwardly prayed that was true, daring to believe it. 'Things seem to have turned around. I have Belinda, and that makes it a bit easier to face up to what's happened.'

'So do you think Belinda is the one?'

'I'm hoping so, for Robbie's sake. He likes her and he needs some stability. I don't want to confuse him by bringing different women round now Roisin's not here. For now, he thinks she's the childminder—doesn't know we're together. I think it would be too much for him to take in.'

'He knows about Roisin and Hugh though, doesn't he?'

'Yeah, I s'pose. I just don't want to confuse him.' George drank some beer. 'Have you bumped into Jess and Tom since the argument?'

'Yeah, saw them in the pub yesterday. I waved at them and Tom waved back, didn't smile. Jess ignored me. Cow. Typical woman: can't forgive and forget, has to carry it around with her. Not that there's anything to forgive; we weren't the ones who did anything wrong.'

'I think they'll come round eventually. We've been friends for a long time.'

'That reminds me. I did a Facebook search and I found Petula.'

'Wow! I didn't think you'd actually go through with it.'

Glen looked at his hands.

'So, when are you meeting her? What did you find out?'

'I think she's playing hard to get; you know what women are like.'

'What do you mean?'

'I sent her a message and she replied saying she remembered me; then I suggested we meet up, and she never replied. I thought maybe she had to get off the Internet, or something.'

'Yeah, to go and feed her five children.' George chuckled.

'Anyhow, I've sent her a friend request and I'll take it from there.'

'Don't get your hopes up, Glen. Fifteen years is a long time.'

'You hear stories all the time about people getting back together with their first loves.'

'Just don't expect too much.'

Chapter Thirty-Two

'I suppose you think it's funny?' said Roisin over the phone before she'd even said hello.

George blinked and sat up in bed looking at the time on his phone, then placed it back on his ear.

'It's typical of you, George: childish and insane.'

'Do you have any idea what time it is?'

He turned to look at Belinda, who was somehow still in a deep sleep.

'It's morning,' said Roisin, 'and I'm outside the house. I expect you to come over immediately and do something about it.'

'I have no idea what you're on about.' A black mood descended as he spoke. His fear that Rex could return at any time and start meddling in his life, never went away. He'd thought his life was starting to settle into a comfortable pattern but here it was again, a reminder of the past.

'I'm at the house. Eight Goldfern Road. The one me and Hugh are buying.'

'I haven't been to that house recently. Whatever's happened, it's nothing to do with me.'

'Recently? So you admit you've been here. Why were you here?'

George felt the blood drain from his face. 'Um... when you told me where you were moving to, I visited—wanted to make sure it was suitable for Robbie.' Would she believe that?

'Let's get one thing straight, George: you and I are over. I'm with Hugh now. If me and Hugh think a house is suitable for Robbie, then it is. We don't need you meddling.'

'Meddling? He's my son. I have rights. You were going on at me for employing a childminder without telling you.'

'That's different.'

'I don't have time for this.' George sighed. 'It's seven o'clock on a Saturday morning, why are you phoning me?'

'We have a viewing. We want to sell this shithole. We were coming to make sure it looked presentable, and now this!'

'What?'

'I have no idea why you're doing this, George; if it's because you don't want me to take Robbie to live with me, so you're trying to delay me being able to buy a new house with Hugh—'

'I haven't done anything!'

'Of all things, spiders. You know I hate spiders. It's because I told you what the neighbour said about the house, isn't it? You're a complete bastard, do you know that? I'm warning you: if you don't get this sorted out, I'll instruct my solicitor to ask for more money from the sale of our house to make up for the cost of dealing with this. And don't think I'll play fair with the childcare arrangements either; I'll make it hell for you, George!'

He listened silently. After hearing "spiders" he'd gone blank. *Rex is back.*

'Spiders?' he said.

'The place is infested! I have a young couple coming to view in two hours. I need this place cleaned.'

'Spiders?'

'George. Get here now.'

George heard the line go dead and slowly took the phone away from his ear. It didn't make sense. Why would Rex be causing problems? Perhaps it was as simple as he was a ghost who was now haunting the house: it might not have anything to do with revenge. Or the house being infested with spiders might be nothing more than a strange coincidence.

Things had reverted to almost normal in the past

couple of months. George had dared to believe it was over and that in time the horrific events that haunted his mind would slowly fade to nothing. He'd mulled it over and concluded that everything he'd experienced since—the nightmares, visions, etc.—was borne out of his own paranoia because he'd been the one to burn down the house. The more he'd pondered it, the more he'd been able to convince himself that the paranormal disturbances had only ever existed in his imagination. Even when Glen turned into a spider before his eyes, he told himself it was possible he'd imagined it.

What bothered him most was that both he and Glen had witnessed Roisin and Hugh becoming spiders and there seemed to be no logical explanation. He thought of Glen's ridiculous theory, the "multiple effect", and somewhere deep inside wished it could be explained away so easily. The more rational part of his brain was stumped, however, and he couldn't shift the sinister sensation that was evoked by reminders of Rex.

Roisin's phone call had brought the horror back. *'I've got you in my web.'* The voice resounded in his head. Was it all in his head, or had *The Spider* returned?

Chapter Thirty-Three

Jess lay in bed staring up at the ceiling of the flat she shared with Tom. It was seven o'clock, Saturday morning. It would have been done by now. She couldn't help the smile that spread across her lips. Her brother said the shipment of spiders would be easy to arrange: his friend worked for an online company that sold all sorts of spiders as pets.

She wanted to teach Glen and George a lesson. Even though they were well aware that Tom was unemployed when they'd inherited the house on Goldfern Road, and she'd had to work hard for minimum wage for years, they weren't willing to give them even a tiny share of the money from the house sale. She'd considered them good friends up until that point. Money changes people—that's what she'd always been told. She'd never imagined that two of her best friends would become so shallow and selfish after coming into money. All she and Tom had wanted was a bit of help until they were back on their feet. Their friends' betrayal had deeply offended her.

She'd noticed the estate agent's board still up outside the house by chance when she was passing by the street, in a taxi, on her way to a hospital appointment. Her intention was to scupper any chance of a sale. She'd considered throwing a brick through the window, or setting the place on fire, but didn't want to end up in prison. Spiders. The perfect solution. Her brother said his friend could deliver on Friday in the middle of the night. He said he'd deliver them through the letterbox.

'Spiders?' Glen shouted over the phone. 'You woke me up to tell me about spiders? It's got nothing to do with me!'

The phone line went dead and George held his head. He didn't want to face going to the house.

While having a shower, it suddenly occurred to him that none of it was his fault. Fuelled by this thought, he dried himself off, went into the bedroom, and grabbed his mobile. Taking it out onto the landing, so as not to wake Belinda, he looked up Roisin's name in his contacts wishing he could delete her from the phone and his life, and cursing the fact that they had to stay in touch for Robbie's sake.

'Hi,' he said when she answered. 'I'm calling to tell you I'm not coming over. It's nothing to do with me if your house is infested with spiders. You deal with it.' He clicked the "end call" button and a few seconds later her name flashed up again as she rang back. He clicked "reject" and put the phone into his pocket, then went downstairs to make breakfast.

'Do what you want, Rex,' he said to no one in particular, wondering if the ghost was around to hear him. 'You'll never win.'

Chapter Thirty-Four

Petula logged on to Facebook almost fearfully. It had been about two weeks since she'd chatted with Ebony online, and a couple of days since she'd last been online and found the message from Glen. What surprises would be waiting for her today?

There were two notifications, a friend request, and one message.

She clicked on the message first, holding her breath. It was from Ebony.

Hi Petula. Where are you? Haven't seen you on Facebook for a week or so. How was the trip to Cambridge? Hope you're ok. Ebony.

Petula hesitated before replying.

Hi Ebony. I'm fine thanks. I've been busy looking for work and didn't want to be distracted by Facebook! I hope you and the girls are ok. Pet x

She felt relieved there were no more messages from Glen and half-heartedly clicked on the notifications, not expecting anything other than someone having "liked" one of her photos. She saw that, as predicted, there were two likes for her recent photos.

Then she clicked on the friend request, reluctantly; usually it'd be a stranger and she just deleted them. Somehow, though, she already knew before she clicked on it who it was from, and perhaps that was why she'd left it till last. A friend request from Glen.

Her mouse arrow hovered over the delete button, but

she couldn't do it. Exhaling deeply, she clicked on "Confirm Request".

Petula's Facebook page held no clues as to her actual life and she preferred it that way. She painted herself as a successful artist and photographer. She'd told Ebony she worked a day job as a waitress at a local café and took photographs in her spare time. She'd created a whole other person, Petula the artist/photographer, and she enjoyed weaving interesting stories about what this fictional Petula got up to. Her alter ego lived an adventurous life. Petula often thought her real talent lie in creative writing.

Adding Glen as a friend wouldn't be too much of a problem, she surmised. Nothing on her page indicated where she lived and nothing revealed her as a petty criminal who'd recently spent time in jail. Glen would think she was a talented photographer.

Another message appeared. A reply from Ebony.

I didn't know you were looking for another job. Hope the search goes well ☺

Petula Replied: **Thanks, Ebony x**

She stood up and peered at herself in the mirror. Today was the day she'd implement the changes needed to start her life again. She looked at the clock. She was due at the job centre in less than an hour.

Chapter Thirty-Five

George met Glen in the pub at lunchtime.

'You look like the cat who got the cream,' said George, morosely, noticing the big grin on Glen's face.

'You'll never guess what happened, but first let's order lunch and I'll tell you all about it.'

They sat down to their pie and chips, and Glen frowned. 'Before I tell you my news, sorry about Saturday, but I'm not a morning person and when you mentioned spiders it freaked me out.'

'No problem,' said George, 'I told Roisin she should deal with it herself. I'm sick of her blaming me for everything; she's the one who had an affair.'

'Good for you, mate.' Glen sipped his beer. 'Why did she even think it had anything to do with you? I thought you kept Rex and the house a secret from her.'

'I did, but she seems to think I'm trying to stop her buying a house with Hugh and that I don't want Robbie to live with them.'

'Well, you don't.'

'I know, but I wouldn't do anything like that. I'm over Roisin. She can do what she wants; I've got Belinda now.'

'Yeah, the elusive Belinda. I'm starting to think you made her up. We'll have to arrange a double-date soon.' He grinned.

'A double-date?'

'Petula accepted my friend request.'

George raised his eyebrows.

'Her relationship status says she's single. I told you there was a reason I wanted to find her.'

'What is she doing these days?'

'She's uploaded lots of photos on her page; I think

she's some kind of photographer. Really great pictures.'

'Are you gonna meet up?'

'I haven't had time to chat with her yet.'

'Don't get your hopes up.'

'Stop being so negative. I have a good feeling about this.'

'Going back to your ex?'

'What's wrong with it? People do it all the time. And we were young; we didn't know what we were doing back then.'

'I hope it works out for you.'

'Thanks.'

'Listen, Glen, about the house and the spider infestation.'

'What happened there?'

'I'm not sure. Roisin phoned saying it was infested with spiders. Who could've done that?'

'You don't think it was Rex, do you? That would be... freaky.'

George pushed away the dark thoughts that threatened to overwhelm him. 'It just seems like a bit of a coincidence that it was spiders.'

'Sounds like a practical joke. Loads of people knew Rex used to dress up as a spider. Could have been kids having a laugh.'

'Maybe.' George battled with his fear.

'Look, as you said, it's none of our business, not our problem. Let Roisin and Hugh sort it out.'

'Yeah.'

Tom appeared at the table. 'Hello,' he said, almost apologetically. 'Can I join you?'

Glen glanced at his watch. 'We came for lunch. We're leaving soon.'

'Yes, take a seat,' said George, ignoring Glen, wishing

once again that things could go back to the way they were before Rex and 8 Goldfern Road turned his life upside down.

'Thanks.' Tom sat on a stool. 'I wanted to apologise.'

'Water under the bridge,' said George. 'We've been friends for years, right? Let's just put it behind us.'

'I'm not talking about our argument. It's something else.' Tom appeared pensive.

George looked at him blankly.

Glen shook his head as if he didn't understand.

'It's about the spiders.' Tom lowered his eyes. 'I had a massive row with Jess.'

'Jess?' George said.

'Yeah, sorry. She ordered the spiders. She told me this morning, thinking I'd be pleased. It was a kind of revenge for what you did... The argument. She wanted to make it harder for you to sell the property. She shouldn't have done it.'

'Jess put the spiders in the house?' George said, relief washing over him. He began to laugh.

Tom looked from George to Glen in bemusement.

'We thought it was... Oh, never mind,' said Glen, smiling at Tom. 'Thanks for telling us.'

'Tell Jess not to worry,' said George, cheerfully.

'I-I, okay... I thought you'd be angry.'

'We don't have anything to do with the house anymore,' explained George. 'We gave the sale proceeds to the executors. We didn't want anything from that weird spider-man. It was making us tense, you know? We kept having nightmares and stuff.'

'George was having nightmares,' clarified Glen.

Tom nodded. 'I see. Wow. Right. I'll tell Jess.'

'Hey, why don't we meet tonight for drinks? Bring Jess. It's about time we all put the past behind us,' suggested George.

Tom smiled and bowed his head as he left the pub.

'Can you believe that?' said George when Tom had gone.

'Yeah, Jess is a right bitch, ain't she? I told you, didn't I?'

George waved his hand, 'No. I mean, it wasn't The Spider... It wasn't Rex. You know what that means, don't you? It means we're free. I haven't had any nightmares for ages. He must have gone at last, you know, wherever people go when they're dead.'

'Yeah, I s'pose you're right. To be honest, I haven't given him much thought recently. Been too busy with other things.'

'Me too, but it was still there at the back of my mind, you know.'

'You need to learn to let stuff go.'

'Huh, says the man who's held on to his memories of Petula for a lifetime.'

'Well, that seems to have worked out for the best.'

'Hmm.'

'I still can't believe what Jess did,' said Glen, shaking his head.

'She was upset.'

'Yeah, but she thought we were getting the sale proceeds and she wanted to jeopardise any sales. Bitch.'

'Look, be nice to her tonight. We need to try and put it all behind us.' George sipped his beer. 'Hey, didn't Jess know Petula at uni? I'm sure those two were friends. You can ask if she keeps in touch with her. She might have some more information about what she's been up to for the past fifteen years.'

Chapter Thirty-Six

Petula took a shower in the cold water. The boiler wasn't working and even though she'd complained to the landlord, no one did anything about it. Cursing her luck, she tried to think positively. She wondered where Glen lived. Perhaps he had a lovely big house with functioning hot water. He might even have a garden. The image of a beautiful house in the countryside flashed into her mind's eye, like the ones she'd seen on *Escape to the Country*: a thatched cottage, with acres of land. She'd be able to take lots of great photographs of the flora and fauna. Glen might have a good job and be able to support her until she could set up her own photography business.

She felt almost as if she were walking on air, buoyed by her dreams as she left her flat on the way to the job centre. Passing by a charity shop, she made a mental note to return there after signing-on; she needed some new clothes. She stopped in front of a hairdressing salon and looked at the price list displayed in the window. *I can afford a haircut if I only buy the bare minimum groceries.*

Her sights were set on starting a new life with Glen. He'd been such a nice boy; would he still be as nice as a man? Time changed people. So many years had passed between them. He may have been married and divorced, or was he still married? She'd forgotten to check his Facebook status. What if he only wanted to be friends? She may have read too much into him wanting to meet her. She'd already begun to imagine a perfect life with Glen, but what if he wasn't available? A frown settled on her brow as she stepped into the main entrance at the job centre. She took her place in the queue and waited.

Petula breezed out of the job centre and couldn't remember ever feeling so driven. She had done a job search and found a couple of posts advertising for candidates who were able to start immediately. One was a receptionist position at the local doctors' surgery, and the other an administrator role at the library. They were both jobs that she was sure would bore her rigid, having worked similar positions in the past, but it was a start, and she needed to have something to focus on.

Before her first dalliance with drugs, she'd actually had quite a promising job at a solicitors' firm. She had been planning to take a few exams while working, with the aim of becoming a legal executive; her boss offered to fund her training, as she was a hard worker. Then she met Colin and started turning up for work late, became so unreliable that she lost her job.

She put it all to the back of her mind as she stood at the entrance to the hairdressing salon she'd spotted on her way to the job centre. *Today is the first day of the rest of my life,* she thought, smiling to herself.

Chapter Thirty-Seven

'I kept in touch with her for a few years after uni,' said Jess. 'She was working in a solicitors' office; I think she wanted to go into legal work.'

Jess and Tom sat opposite Glen and George in the pub.

'Sounds promising,' said Glen, winking at George and rubbing his hands together.

'But she lost her job,' continued Jess, 'and one of our other friends, Beth, said she was taking drugs.'

'Beth?' said George. 'Beth Little?'

'Yeah, we still keep in touch sometimes,' said Jess.

'Wow, do you keep in touch with any other people from uni?' asked George.

'That can wait,' said Glen, butting in. 'What did you say about Petula taking drugs?'

Jess shrugged, and said, 'I don't know if it's true, but it was a rumour. Beth saw her with a man at a local pub and she tried to say hello, but Petula looked drunk, and Beth saw Petula's boyfriend—or who she assumed was her boyfriend— dealing drugs later that evening outside the pub.'

'She lived in a council estate last time we saw her, didn't she?' said Tom.

'Yeah. I visited her there once, quite a nice little flat. I'm not sure if she still lives there. We used to exchange Christmas cards but stopped about ten years ago.'

'Do you still have her address?' asked Glen, leaning forward.

'Five, Peppercorn Mansions, in Camden. I can't remember the postcode.'

'Why are you asking about Petula now? Didn't you two used to date at one time?' asked Tom.

'Yeah.' Glen nodded. 'I recently hooked up with her

again on Facebook.'

'Me and Jess opened Facebook accounts a while back, but we never use them,' said Tom.

'I don't use it,' said George.

'I don't usually use it,' said Glen, 'but it's a great way to track down people you used to know. From what I've seen of her Facebook page, she's a photographer now,' he added.

'Wow,' Jess gushed. 'I might take a look at that. I've always liked taking photos.'

'Yeah, Jess has a few hundred photos on our computer at home. Great shots.'

'Yeah, but Petula takes professional ones, not like your amateur photography.'

'It's not amateur, actually,' said Jess. 'I won a prize for one of my photos.'

'What, when you were in school?' ribbed Glen.

'No, it was a photography magazine competition.'

'That's probably because no one else entered.'

'There were thousands of entries.'

'He's only winding you up, Jess,' said Tom.

'You and Petula have lots in common, Jess,' said George. 'You should get back in touch with her.'

'I'm meeting up with her soon,' interjected Glen.

'I thought she didn't get back to you.' George raised an eyebrow.

'She did. We've arranged a date. So I'll ask her if she wants to meet up with you lot again.'

'That would be nice,' said Tom. 'I've lost touch with everyone from uni. Apart from you two.'

'I exchange birthday and Christmas cards with Beth,' said Jess, 'and I sometimes see Susan. Do you remember Susan Frost?'

'Oh, my God, yeah; the girl with the thick glasses.' Glen chuckled.

'She wears contacts now,' Jess said pointedly. 'Why do you have to be so cruel about what women look like?'

'I'm not. I've never said anything about what you look like, have I?'

She narrowed her eyes at him.

'It proves I can be nice sometimes. There are a lot of things I *could* say, but I don't.'

'You're so childish.'

'Sorry to interrupt the scintillating conversation, but I've gotta go,' said George, standing up. 'I'm having dinner with Belinda tonight. I'm glad we're all back on speaking terms now.'

'When do we get to meet Belinda?' asked Tom.

'Soon,' replied George, smiling.

'I'm off, too,' said Glen. 'I have a date with Facebook.' He winked.

Chapter Thirty-Eight

'*I want to make a deal with you.*' The familiar voice resounded.

George jumped. He was all alone in his kitchen, unable to sleep and not entirely sure why, so he'd sneaked down to the kitchen to make a warm drink. He almost spilt his drink on hearing the voice. *Rex?*

'*I can't wait for you to have a second child. I need to complete my mission sooner. Your girlfriend is pregnant, but it's not your child. She's sleeping with Fernando from the pub where she works in the evening. He's her real boyfriend. She's only using you. She wanted the money from my estate.*'

George spun around in his chair, not sure what he was looking for. Hoping he was dreaming, he whispered, 'Who are you?'

'*I don't have time to play games, George. I thought that if I could be reborn into another human body I could achieve everything I wanted, but something that happened has made me see another way.*'

'You're not real, you're a figment of my imagination, a symptom of post-traumatic stress disorder, a dream...'

'*Keep fooling yourself, George. I am The Spider and I will win. I've got you in my web, but it's not enough. I saw the spiders at my house. So magnificent. There were so many of them; a multitude of magnificence—I should have been a poet. You know, the problem was that in my time on earth, as was the case with so many prophets before me, no one understood; no one could fathom my extraordinary greatness. That's why I must now claim my glory; that which is rightfully mine. I must prove they were wrong. I knew straight away when I saw those arachnids that it was a sign.*

'*No more will I wait to be reborn into the body of a lowly human when I can become a real spider. If I could possess the body of a deadly spider, I will have achieved a lifelong dream. It's not enough to dress like one, I have to be one.*'

'Wh-why are you telling me this?'

'Those spiders were not poisonous, they were the kind you buy as pets over the Internet. I want to be a poisonous spider, George. This could work for both of us.'

'What? What do you mean?'

'As I said before, I want to make a deal with you.'

'What deal?'

'I need to possess a spider's body. I need a poisonous spider. You must get me a deadly one.'

'I don't know where to get them.'

'Do this for me and I'll leave you alone.'

'B-but who will you kill?'

'Do this for me, George. If you don't, I swear I will kill you.'

'How do I know you won't kill me when you turn into a poisonous spider?'

'You don't.'

'So why should I do it?'

'Because if you don't I will kill you anyway. It may take longer, but I will do it.'

'If I do this for you, I'll be helping you achieve a lifelong dream, right? If you never died in the first place, you wouldn't have been able to become a spider. So, if I do this, I need you to promise you'll leave me and my family alone.'

'You have my word.'

George took a deep breath. 'Okay, okay, give me a few days. I have to find out how I can get a spider. Wait. Where shall I leave it?'

'At my house, of course.'

'But... But they're selling it. What if they see me?'

'Leave it there at night. Make sure you do it. This could be your way out, or the worst decision you ever made. Your choice.'

The next morning, George woke up and wondered if it had all been a dream. Had Rex actually offered him a deal?

He turned over onto his side and saw Belinda coming out of the en-suite.

'You're awake at last,' she said.

'Wh-what's the time?'

'It's about eight. I'll wake Robbie up and get him ready for school.'

George looked at Belinda's tummy as she pulled on her jeans. She didn't appear to be pregnant. It was absurd: how could he believe an incorporeal voice that might have just been his imagination running away with him? *But it seemed so real.*

'When you get back from the school run, we'll have a nice breakfast,' he said. 'I'll make pancakes.'

'That would've been nice, but maybe another time. I'll grab something to eat on my way out. I have to go and see my mum today; she's not well.'

'Sorry to hear that. What's wrong with her?'

'Sounds like flu. Look, we can have dinner later, if my mum's better, yeah? Um... you'll have to collect Robbie from school because I'm not sure how long I'll be at my mum's house.'

'Right,' said George.

When Belinda left the room, George sat up in bed. His mind would not rest. Was she cheating on him? He had to follow her, had to find out.

As he approached the en-suite, he heard her laughing with Robbie in the main bathroom and that made him angry. She wasn't only playing with his heart but his son's. If he found out that she was cheating on him he'd have to fire her, and Robbie would be upset as he'd grown close to her.

It was a dream. He splashed water on his face,

deliberately using cold water in the hope that the iciness might somehow wake him up, shock him out of the density of his deep thoughts. *Only a dream.*

After waiting for Belinda and Robbie to leave the house and walk up to the end of the street, he sent a text to his secretary at work to let her know he'd be late, and jumped into his car. He drove to the school gates, parking up a few metres away.

Shortly, Belinda exited the school gates, waving behind her to Robbie. She crossed the road and strolled along the avenue. George followed in the car, slowly.

When Belinda reached a bus stop, she stood there and took her mobile from her pocket. George watched on from across the road in his car. Soon it appeared that she might be chatting by text: every so often she smiled at the screen. He wished he was able to get closer, unable to see her expression clearly.

A bus pulled up and when it left the bus stop Belinda had gone.

George followed the bus. At each stop, he tried to stay behind the vehicle, but sometimes it wasn't possible because the designated bus lanes forced him to drive ahead, then he'd have to wait in a side road for the bus to reappear, making it impossible for him to tell whether Belinda had got off at one of the earlier stops. He began to feel foolish.

As he was about to try to turn the car around and head to work, he saw Belinda jump off the bus. Now very close to her, he became worried she would spot him, but she headed in the opposite direction towards the busy high street.

Searching around for a convenient place to park, George noticed a side road. He pulled into the residential street, parked up, and then hurried out, almost forgetting in his haste to lock the car.

Belinda was still in sight as he reached the main road,

then she proceeded left into another street. He ran to catch up, but stayed a few feet behind her, then watched her go up some steps leading to a house.

He'd never visited her parents' house before. She'd told him her parents lived in Hertfordshire in a lovely cottage. This wasn't Hertfordshire, or a cottage. This terraced house looked as though it might have been converted into flats.

George hovered around outside for a moment. He'd been to Belinda's own flat a couple of times and this wasn't it.

At the end of the street, he noted the name, Berger Road. It didn't mean anything to him.

As he sat on one of the garden walls further down the street, it occurred to him that he'd followed her here because of what must have been a dream, the words of a dead man accusing her of having an affair. *It's all in my mind.* It felt as if he'd only now woken up and realised this. Leaning forward, he held his head. *What the hell am I doing?*

He stood up and made his way towards the high street, seriously starting to worry about the state of his mental health. *Maybe Glen's right. Maybe I should see a therapist.*

Just then, his phone rang.

'Hi, George.'

Belinda's voice.

Panic gripped him. Had she spotted him? How could he explain following her? She'd be upset, knowing he didn't trust her. He cursed Roisin for cheating on him; would this be what it was like from now on? Would he ever be able to trust another woman?

'Hello.'

'Listen, I have to stay overnight with my mum. She's not well at all. My dad is finding it hard to cope.'

His thoughts raced and fluctuated between wanting to scream at her for lying to him, and feeling terrible for thinking she'd been having an affair if all the while her mum was unwell. 'I'm sorry to hear that, Bel, I hope she gets well soon.'

'Me too. I'm making her some soup, and I'll stay with her while my dad catches up on sleep. Last night was difficult for him because she couldn't sleep.'

'Oh, dear. Listen, keep me posted and let me know if there's anything I can do to help.'

'I will. I'll try and get back in time to take Robbie to school tomorrow.'

'No, it's all right, don't rush, I can arrange that.'

'Thanks. Hopefully see you sometime tomorrow.'

George placed his mobile back in his pocket. She had sounded a bit breathless, as if trying to hold back tears. He turned back to face the house, debating whether to go there, offer help. No; if he did that, she would know he'd followed her.

Just then, Belinda exited the house holding hands with a man.

Fernando?

The giggling couple got into a car.

It can't be true, thought George.

'So when are you gonna break up with him?' asked Fernando as he put the car into gear.

'Soon. I feel sorry for his son. I don't want to lose my job there,' replied Belinda.

'Smooth that you still get paid for looking after his son even though you're supposed to be in a relationship.'

Belinda smiled. 'It's easy to twist older men around your little finger. I learned that years ago.'

'I bet you did.'

'Hey.' Belinda punched his arm. 'I'm not a slut. This was as much your idea as mine.'

'I know, but what you're doing at the moment is a bit wrong though, isn't it? And I don't like the idea of you sleeping in the same bed as him.'

'We don't sleep together anymore; well, I mean, we don't have sex. I only did that when I thought he'd inherit that money. I'm a one-man woman Fernando. I've been doing this for us.'

'Good to hear it.'

'I'll break it off soon.'

'I was starting to think you were falling in love with him.'

'I hope he hasn't guessed anything,' she said, her brow creased in thought.

'Why would he?'

'You were kissing me when I was on the phone; what did my voice sound like?'

'I'm sure he didn't guess, and so what if he did? You've gotta break it off with him. He's not worth anything to us now.'

'Next time, leave me alone when I'm speaking to him, yeah? I need to tell him in my own time.'

'I won't wait for ever, Bel. If you don't tell him, I will.'

When George got back from his escapade, following Belinda halfway around London, he called his boss and said that Robbie was ill and he had no one to look after him. After that, he ended up milling around the house, thinking about what had gone wrong in his life. In an attempt to stop himself falling into a downward spiral of gloom, he switched on the television. The cheery presenters on the shows only managed to wind him up. They looked far too happy and that served to exacerbate his feeling that he was the only person going through hell. He knew it was ridiculous to think that, but the weight on his mind just would not shift.

When he collected Robbie from school, the first words from the child's lips were, 'Where's Belinda?'

George felt his anger rise again at how Belinda had toyed with his affections oblivious of how this would affect Robbie. Plastering a smile to his face, he answered with, 'She had to work, Robbie. Listen, son, how would you like to stay over at your gran and granddad's house tonight?'

'Can I bring my dinosaur?'

'Yes, of course.'

George had phoned his father earlier that day. His parents lived on the other side of town, but he knew they wouldn't turn down a chance to spend time with Robbie.

'We'd love to have Robbie to stay,' his dad had said. 'You should bring him round more often.'

'I know. Sorry, Dad; I've been busy with work.'

'How's Roisin?'

'Um... she's fine.'

'I suppose you two want to spend some time alone together. Where are you going? Anywhere nice?'

'Out to dinner,' lied George. He felt terrible lying to his dad, but the truth wasn't something he had time to talk about and he knew it would only upset his parents.

'That's nice. You should spend time together. It helps. It can be hard when you're bringing up a young one. Your mother and I are happy to help out, whenever you need us. We'll see you later.'

'Thanks, Dad.'

He'd regretted asking his dad as soon as he put the

phone down, knowing Robbie would most likely tell them everything about how Roisin no longer lived at the house and he'd definitely mention Belinda... and probably Hugh.

'So, how was school?' asked George as he ushered Robbie to the car.

'School's boring,' said Robbie. 'Daddy, can I have a biscuit?'

George's head was spinning. He settled Robbie into the car seat and gave him a couple of biscuits. 'Robbie, when you go to Grandma and Granddad's house tonight don't tell them that Mummy doesn't live at home, all right? It's a secret and they don't know.'

'I can keep secrets,' said Robbie whilst chewing a biscuit.

'If you do keep the secret I'll give you some more biscuits when I collect you.'

'Can I have the chocolate ones?'

'Yes, chocolate.'

George sat in the driver's seat his mind abuzz with conflicting thoughts. It was too late to ask anyone else to look after Robbie. Who could he ask, anyway? Glen didn't know the first thing about childcare, and he didn't want to ask Roisin if she'd take him; that would only give her more ammunition to use in the court proceedings about where Robbie should live.

After dropping Robbie off at his parents' house, George drove along the motorway, heading towards the pub where Belinda worked.

Chapter Thirty-Nine

Glen got off the Tube at Camden Town and consulted the map he'd downloaded from the Internet. Peppercorn Mansions wasn't far from the station, according to the map. He walked along the high street, nervous but full of anticipation.

He'd sent another Facebook message to Petula the night before, asking if they could meet up.

That would be so great, Glen. I'd love to see you again, but I'm really busy these days. I'll let you know when I can find a free half hour and we'll go for a coffee, ok?

He took this to mean that she wanted to meet up with him but was a bit nervous because so many years had passed between them. He didn't want to waste any more time, though. He'd been thinking about her over the years and all his subsequent relationships were tainted by recollections of Petula. She had been everything he'd imagined his dream girl would be. Long blonde hair, bluest of blue eyes, and dressed in up-to-the-minute fashion with flawless make-up and smelling of the latest perfume. None of the other girls he'd dated over the years ever compared to his perfect girl.

The rumour about Petula being involved with drugs sounded insane to him. When they were dating, she'd been so anti-drugs. Once, at a party, they'd been offered an "E" by a fellow student. Petula had lectured the boy about how drugs could kill him, and she'd sent him away.

As Glen approached the council estate, he told himself to remember that she was older now, and he didn't know for sure whether she was in a relationship, married, or even whether she had children. He took a deep breath as he entered the estate grounds.

🕷

Petula observed her reflection in the mirror and smiled. A new, improved version of herself smiled back. Her hair looked much better. The hairdresser suggested she dye her hair because there were signs of grey. She'd given her a shoulder-length style and Petula had decided to change her natural colour. When younger, she'd experimented with colour and remembered that she'd liked having jet black hair, as it complemented her pale skin and blue eyes.

The style and the colour suited her, but taking a closer look at her face she frowned, noticing the wrinkles. It had been years since she'd worn make-up; currently she didn't own any make-up. She resolved to buy some lipstick, at least, when she was next out, and considered buying an anti-wrinkle cream.

After taking a shower, Petula reached into the plastic carrier bag she'd been given at the charity shop, and took out the new top and trousers she'd bought. They were not exactly her style, but they were a bargain, and the plum colour of the trousers went well with the pink of the top.

She put on her new clothes and looked in the mirror. For some reason, thoughts of Glen sprang to mind. The woman in the mirror was definitely a far cry from the pretty young girl she'd been at university; what would he think of her now? Back then she wore designer clothes and lots of accessories. She'd sold all her jewellery years ago, to feed her drug habit.

Slipping into her worn-out black pumps, Petula felt disappointed that they didn't suit her outfit at all, but they were the only shoes she owned and would have to do. Having run out of money yesterday, she couldn't do anything about it. Hopefully, her attire was smart enough for the job interview: they weren't interviewing her for a professional or customer-service role, so her appearance wouldn't be a top priority.

She grabbed her bag and was about to head out of the door when the doorbell rang.

Taking one final glance in the mirror, she went over to the door and opened it. Outside stood a man who looked familiar. Her hand went to her mouth as realisation struck: *Glen.*

Glen wondered if he'd got the address wrong. 'Uh... this is number five, isn't it?' he said, taking in the scrawny woman with jet black hair.

'What are you doing here, and how did you get my address?'

Oh my God. Petula.

Glen stood dumbfounded. This was Petula? She looked nothing like herself. She appeared annoyed, or upset... Were those tears in her eyes? 'I'm sorry, maybe I shouldn't have come,' he said, eager to leave, cursing himself for wasting energy thinking about this woman.

'You definitely shouldn't have come here.' Anger reddened her cheeks as she stepped out of the flat. 'I'm on my way to a job interview. I can't be late.'

Her voice was the same, and he recalled her feistiness in the way she chided him. She closed her front door and hurried away towards the stairs.

He watched on as this woman, his dream girl who was nothing like his dream girl, disappeared around the corner.

How could I have been so stupid? he thought. *Of course she'd be different.* He tried to catch another glimpse of her as he followed down the stairs. *She's older. She's dyed her hair, but she's still Petula.*

'Are you following me?' she said abruptly, spinning around to face him.

He held up his hands. 'No. I'm just leaving.'

She stood as if waiting for him to catch up to her.

He walked hesitantly towards her.

'Listen,' she said, wiping her nose. 'I didn't expect to see you today. I didn't mean to be rude. If you want to meet for a coffee sometime that would be great.'

He stared at her half-smile. She looked nervous, almost shaking. Was she on drugs? She looked like she might be... She was very skinny.

'I could take you out to dinner,' he said. 'My treat.'

Her smile grew, and as her cheeks coloured with joy he was reminded of the young girl she'd once been. Her blue-blue eyes reflected the sun and brought forth memories of the times they'd spent together. A desire to hug her swept over him, but she appeared so fragile.

'You haven't changed, Glen. You're still so handsome.' She grinned. 'Why did I let you get away, hey?'

At first he stared blankly, unsure how to react. If she was anyone else, looking as she did now, he wouldn't have given her the time of day. It was all about looks with him, and what kind of body a woman had. Something clicked in his head, and he felt an emotion with no name. Petula wasn't pretty—time had taken that away—and she was rake thin; but his feelings hadn't changed. He still cared. Smiling at her, he said, 'I've never forgotten you, Petula.'

She glanced at her watch. 'I have to go or I'll be late, but message me on Facebook, yeah? We'll meet up for dinner. I'd love that.'

They swapped phone numbers and he watched her leave. He knew then that he still loved her. He'd always loved her and always would.

Later that day, Petula strutted out of the job interview, a huge smile on her face.

She'd sailed through the questions; with her new-found confidence she had won over her potential employer. He'd offered her the job there and then, saying how he thought she'd fit in well at the library.

Petula was happy to finally be free of the job centre and the derogatory comments from the staff there, such as, 'You've been unemployed for a while, Ms Harrigan; you have to make more of an effort.' Many of them, she recalled, often looked down their noses at her when she attended fortnightly to sign and tell them: *Yes*, the job search was going well, but *no*, she hadn't found a job yet. They treated her like a disease, something they had to get rid of, yet they did little to help.

She couldn't wait to tell them that she'd found a job.

Her thoughts turned to Glen; the reason she was in such a buoyant mood to begin with. At first mortified that he'd arrived unannounced at her flat, it now seemed like a godsend. Her confidence level had been at zero for ages, but after seeing him—and his proposal of a date—it was soaring sky high. If she had any credit in her mobile, she would have called him to tell him the good news.

Chapter Forty

George parked his car on a side road and questioned what he hoped to achieve by coming here. Even if Belinda were having an affair with Fernando, they wouldn't be doing anything here in a public bar.

He remembered meeting Fernando once, one Saturday evening when he'd dropped Belinda off at the pub. Fernando was a young man; young and beautiful like Belinda. They made a perfect couple. George clenched his teeth.

He wondered why he hadn't thought of disguising himself. Belinda would see him as soon as he entered the pub. *What am I even doing here?* He felt like an impostor, observing someone else's life, recognising that his dalliance with Belinda was nothing but a desperate fling.

There was no passion in his chase here to the pub; he hadn't been driven by an all-consuming love and didn't want to fight to get Belinda back. Only a numbness existed. She meant nothing to him now; it was his pride that had made him follow her. Their relationship had developed too soon after his marriage fell apart. His battered confidence recovered and his ego was boosted when this young, beautiful woman wanted to be his girlfriend.

But she was playing with him, seeing a younger man on the side. That was the bitter reality. Feeling older than his thirty-seven years, it struck him that he didn't even know how old Belinda was; she'd once mentioned she was born in the nineties, so at most she must be in her mid-twenties.

A man crossed the road in front of where his car was parked, and George began to feel self-conscious, sitting there. He got out of the car and stood there for a while under a streetlamp. He contemplated getting back into the car and driving until everything made sense, until he'd put sufficient distance between them to see more clearly. It was all too much for him; closing in, not leaving him room to breathe.

Remembering there was a baseball cap in the boot, he walked to the back of his car but then realised the pointlessness of thinking a disguise like that could work. Shaking his head, he locked the car.

He'd come all this way with the intention of finding Belinda in the pub and confronting her if Fernando was there. It all seemed so silly now. Blindly, and not knowing why he was continuing with this game, George trundled along the high street.

Belinda had said she'd be with her mother today: if she'd been telling the truth she wouldn't even be working. Maybe that was the proof he needed: if he went in and she wasn't there. Could that be what he was hoping to find? There was no denying what he'd witnessed earlier though; the way she had smiled and laughed as she held hands with Fernando. That image had burrowed deep into George's brain.

Trying to formulate a plan, his mind whirred: *If they are both in there, I'll wait until closing time, wait until they leave, see if they leave together, follow...* He pondered the futility of it all.

After seeing them together earlier, what further proof did he need? Why bother with this? Just to feel more pain? Had he developed an appetite for self-destruction?

The pub was quite busy. The bustle and noise came as a bit of a shock to George after his quiet drive alone with his thoughts. He saw Belinda behind the bar, distracted, serving a customer. Fernando was not around.

George made his way to the other side of the pub and chose a table in the corner. There was a newspaper on the table, so he picked it up and pretended to read it for a few minutes, but he began to feel conspicuous without a drink.

A pretty young woman, perhaps Belinda's age, joined him at the table. 'Is this seat taken?' she asked, indicating the stool opposite him.

'No,' he said, immediately regretting it, and then hid behind his newspaper again.

'Haven't seen you in here before,' said the woman, placing her drink on the table.

George lowered the newspaper and said, 'No, I'm meeting a business acquaintance. I'm not from around here.'

Why was she talking to him? Had Belinda sent her over? Paranoia took hold.

The woman smiled at him and opened her mouth, about to say something else.

'Excuse me,' he said, then headed for the men's toilets.

On entering the toilets, he felt relieved to find no one else in there and stood for a moment unsure what to do next. Fernando didn't appear to be working this evening, and even if he was, what kind of evidence would that be of an affair?

Sighing to himself, George made the decision to leave and confront Belinda about it the next time they were alone together.

He'd left Robbie at his parents' house, so was free to spend the evening doing what he wanted—why waste it trying to catch out his errant girlfriend, a girlfriend who no longer meant anything to him?

On exiting the toilets he almost bumped into a man. 'Sorry,' he said. When he looked up, he saw Fernando staring back at him.

The boy didn't seem to recognise him at first, but after turning away, gave him a second glance and said, 'Do I know you?'

'No, I don't think so.' George hurried past him.

George glanced back at Belinda as he exited the pub. *She is beautiful, but I was kidding myself,* he thought, walking out of the door. *I never loved her.*

Striding towards his car, he resolved to stay away from women for the foreseeable future, couldn't trust himself not to be duped again. *Perhaps I'll be on my own for ever.*

A sense of isolation gripped him when he got into his car and closed the door behind him. Being alone in the vehicle brought it all home to him. Would this be his life now? No one to share an evening with?

Belinda had filled a hole when Roisin left, and now the hole had opened up again, too big to ignore. He'd believed he and Roisin were unbreakable and would grow old together. Whenever they spoke now there was only bitterness in her voice. She loved Hugh, not him. Belinda's betrayal echoed what had happened with Roisin, as if rubbing salt into a fresh wound. He'd read somewhere that if you kept behaving in a certain way you'd attract the same sort of people and the same pattern of events in your life. Was he unwittingly giving out a signal that it was acceptable to cheat on him, vibrating on that level and somehow attracting the same types of relationships? How could he stop it?

He needed a drink, a friend to talk to.

He phoned Glen.

'Sorry, mate; I've got a date tonight.'

'A date? Who with?'

'Petula.'

'Oh, yeah, you mentioned it in the pub. I thought you were bluffing.'

'Didn't think she'd want to date me? Oh, ye of little faith.'

'I hope it goes well.'

'You sound a bit upset; you all right?'

'Yeah, yeah, I'm fine. Look, we'll talk about it another time.'

'Great. I've gotta go; the cab's waiting outside. I'm taking her to dinner. I have a feeling sometimes love can be better the second time round, y'know. Like age makes you wiser. I'm happier than I've been in a long time.'

'Good. Good to hear it,' said George, tears in his eyes —not because of his friend's news but because his own life had become so hollow.

'We'll catch up soon,' said Glen.

George had no doubt that now Glen had hooked up with Petula again he'd have less time for his friends. It was inevitable.

Another burden weighed down on him, knowing that he was supposed to be looking for a spider for Rex. That man, who wasn't even a man anymore, just a voice, seemed to be controlling him, held power over him.

George started the car and drove away.

Passing by the front of the pub, he saw Belinda outside talking to a man... *Fernando.*

Feeling curious, he pulled up to the kerb—far enough away so that the car wouldn't be noticed by the couple—and sneaked out, hiding behind a large commercial waste bin.

'But honey, he doesn't live round here,' Belinda was saying.

'What if he followed you?'

'Don't be ridiculous.'

'What's ridiculous about it? Maybe he knows about you and me.'

'How?'

'Did you leave your phone lying around in his house?'

'I don't even know why we're having this conversation, Fernando. I'm leaving him. Who cares if he knows about us? I don't give a shit about him.'

'I'm only worried in case he's one of those dudes that would, you know, want to take revenge.'

Belinda giggled. 'Huh! Don't worry! His wife was having sex with the neighbour for months and he didn't do anything to her. In fact, he still loves her; stupid man. I bet he'd take her back if she asked. He's such a loser.'

Silence followed. George assumed they must have gone back into the pub. Peeking around the corner of the bin, he saw them kissing, then went back behind the bin and closed his eyes.

'Promise you'll break it off with him soon; I can't bear the thought of that creep being anywhere near you.'

'Neither can I,' said Belinda. 'He makes me want to puke.'

'C'mon, we better get back inside before the boss finds out we're not there.'

'I love you, Fernando.'

'Love you, too.'

George's mind was in a whirl. He wished he hadn't followed Belinda that morning. He longed to return to the ignorance of believing they were in love. He questioned whether he'd ever really believed that. *I should never have fallen for her. It was on the rebound*, he told himself, as if that would make it easier to deal with the fact that it had ended so sourly. Thoughts of Roisin haunted him. Imagining her with Hugh. Dark thoughts, negative thoughts, clawed at his mind.

All he had succeeded in doing by listening to the young couple outside the pub was adding insult to injury. It would have been better if he'd never heard any of it. It stung. She'd never cared about him. Never. Not even for one moment in time. Belinda had only been after the money from Rex's house.

That damn man and his damn house had cost his marriage and now his dignity.

He felt determined to find the poisonous spider at any

cost and give it to Rex so he could eradicate him from his life once and for all. *I wish he was a real bloody spider. I'd trample him under my feet. If only it were that simple.*

Chapter Forty-One

George drove to Tom and Jess's flat. He hoped they were at home. They usually were, unless they were at the pub. One thing he knew about them was their lifestyle.

At university, everyone guessed Tom and Jess would end up together. From day one, they just seemed like a couple. When all the new students were queueing up outside the main hall waiting for a lecture about the degree course they'd chosen, Tom and Jess stood side by side, both dressed in brown corduroy trousers. Both wore flat brown shoes and navy blue jumpers. It was almost as if they'd been instructed to wear some kind of uniform. They'd laughed about the matching clothing and it broke the ice. For the rest of term they were inseparable. They liked the same music, the same books, and the same films.

Both were gifted students and it came as no surprise when they announced at the beginning of the second term that they were an item.

They used to go out with Glen and George and other friends at university to nightclubs and gigs, but were always happier being on their own, or having a quiet drink in the pub.

Over the years, the couple had become increasingly reclusive, so you could bet money on them being at home if they weren't in the pub.

George pulled up outside the building where Tom and Jess lived.

He mused at how both of them were so brilliant as students but neither of them had fared too well in the job market. Tom had been out of work a few times since leaving university and Jess's track record wasn't much better.

Pressing the intercom buzzer, he waited, unsure of the

reception he'd get, wishing he'd phoned in advance.

Tom answered.

'Hi. It's George. Look, sorry I didn't call you, but I'm kind of in a hurry. Is it all right if I come in?'

'Yeah, no problem, come up.'

Tom met him at the door to the flat. 'Hi, George.' He raised an eyebrow. 'Is everything all right?'

'Um... yeah. Is Jess around?'

'Yeah, she's in the kitchen. I'll get her.'

George followed Tom into the flat and waited in the living room.

'Hi, George,' said Jess, smiling as she entered. 'What's happened?'

'Hi. I'm sorry I came here uninvited, but I have a big favour to ask.'

'Here, sit down,' said Tom, taking a magazine off the sofa to make space.

'Thanks.'

'How can we help?' asked Jess, her brow furrowed.

'I need to know where you got those spiders,' said George.

Jess turned pale.

'Sit down, Jess,' said Tom, taking her by the hand.

She sat next to Tom on the sofa. 'L-look, that was a mistake, but I don't want you to get in trouble about it. Wh-what's happened, are they suing you?'

'No... No, it's nothing like that; I just need to get a spider.'

'Why?' asked Jess and Tom together.

George exhaled deeply. 'You wouldn't believe me if I told you. It's a long story, but I need a poisonous spider—the most deadly kind—as soon as possible.'

'Deadly?' said Jess. 'I got them through a contact that my brother knows, but their website is for pet spiders. They

236

don't have poisonous ones. Aren't they illegal?'

George pleaded with her, 'Your brother's friend must know people if he's in the spider trade; there must be someone who knows how to get poisonous ones.'

'Wh-why on earth would you need such a thing? You're not going to try to kill someone are you, because—'

'No, no! What do you take me for?'

'Sorry, but—'

'Look, let's just say it's for a friend who wants to do an experiment: that's all I can say for now. But it's urgent and it's important.'

'Um... I know that my brother told me about his friend accidentally ordering some poisonous ones a few months ago, but they had to send them back. I'm sure they were illegal. They nearly got fined.'

'So, he must know where to get them. If he's too scared to order it, I can do it myself if you get me the details.'

'No, no; I'm sure he'll do it. But it won't be cheap,' said Jess.

'That doesn't matter.' Running a hand through his hair, he said, 'Get me the spider and I'll pay.'

'Fine. I'll ask him. But no promises.'

'Thanks, Jess.' George felt like hugging her. He was one step closer to freeing himself of *The Spider* once and for all.

Chapter Forty-Two

That evening, Glen took Petula to an Italian restaurant in the heart of London. The food was expensive. Glen, being out to impress, didn't reveal that his cousin owned the restaurant and allowed family to dine for free.

Petula blinked, as if to make sure she wasn't imagining what she was seeing when she read the menu. 'Um... Glen, are you sure we should be eating here? Have you seen these prices? You'd think the food was made of gold! We could get fish 'n' chips, McDonalds? I'm not fussy.'

'Only the best for you, Petula,' said Glen.

She smiled.

Her smile took him back to lazy summer days when they were students with little or no responsibility.

They spent a pleasant evening and, between them, finished off three bottles of wine with their meal.

Glen was feeling tipsy when they left the restaurant. On the way out he said, without much thought, 'Is it true you were a drug addict?' He gulped and immediately regretted asking the question.

'Um... where did you hear that?' Petula glanced at him briefly and appeared to have tears in her eyes. She turned away towards the road. 'I think I'll walk from here. Thanks for the meal.' She began to scurry away.

'No-no, you can't go on your own. It's late.' Glen caught up with her and grabbed her arm.

'I can take care of myself,' she said pulling away.

He walked ahead, then, hearing sniffles, looked back over his shoulder. 'P-Petula, what's wrong? Please don't cry.'

She opened her handbag. 'I haven't got any tissues. Damn.'

Glen reached into his jacket pocket and pulled out a

packet of tissues. 'Here. Let's sit over here and you can tell me what's wrong.' He took her arm and led her to a bus stop.

They sat there under the shelter for a few moments, silently watching the traffic racing past, the lights reflecting off the pavement. It had rained while they were in the restaurant; the ground shone wet under the streetlights.

Petula wiped her nose and said, 'I had a lovely evening, but I don't think it'll work out, will it?'

'What d'you mean? I thought we got on well. Is it because of what I said? I would never had said it; I had a bit too much to drink. It just came out. I—'

'There's no point lying, I suppose,' she said morosely. 'You'd find out eventually.' She stood up and looked down at him. 'Glen, you seem like a nice man, and you've got your life together.' She pointed to the restaurant. 'If you can afford to eat in a place like that, your world is worlds away from mine. I'm lucky to have a pint of milk in my fridge. I'm bad news, and you're better off without me.'

She made to leave.

'Wait, Petula!' He followed. 'Don't go. I've wanted to see you again for so long, and now we're together we should try—'

'What do you mean you've wanted to see me for so long?'

He hung his head. 'I guess I never really got over you. I've been thinking about you over the years and—'

'Huh, I bet you thought I would still be the girl I was back then.'

Glen lowered his gaze. 'Yeah. You're right, I was shocked at how much you've changed and it made me realise I'd been living in a fantasy world for years. You know, no other girl could ever match up to you. I had relationships, but they all failed because none of them were Petula Harrigan.'

Petula's face fell and she held her arms to her sides.

'What did you find so great about me?'

'Everything.'

'Maybe on the outside I looked good.' She ran a hand through her hair and went back to the bus shelter, taking a seat.

He joined her.

'Oh, Glen.' She took his hands in hers. 'I threw it all away, didn't I?'

'I didn't want us to break up; you broke my heart.'

'I know. I'm sorry.' She let go of his hands. 'Look.' She wiped her nose again and gave him the rest of the packet of tissues. 'I meant what I said; you're better off without me.'

'I don't think I am. I'm an ordinary bloke, Petula. This restaurant belongs to my cousin. I could never afford those prices. I brought you here because I wanted it to work out; I wanted you to think I'm better than I am.'

'You're stuck in the past, Glen.' She began to walk away.

'How can you say that?' He stood up. 'What if we're meant to be together?'

'How can we be?' she said, twirling around to face him. 'We split up over fifteen years ago.'

'You remembered how long ago it was.'

'Uh, yes.'

'So it means that you must have been thinking about me on some level over the years.'

'Sorry to disappoint you, but I'd completely forgotten about you until you got in touch on Facebook.'

Glen's hopeful smile faded to a frown. He looked at the ground before speaking again. 'Did you never think back and wonder what happened to me? Didn't you ever wonder what could have happened if we'd stayed together?'

'No. Okay, maybe at the start, and sometimes when I was very lonely. As I say, it's been over fifteen years. We were kids then.'

'Yes, but we've found each other again. It's meant to be.'

'We only found each other because you searched for me on Facebook.'

'Yeah, but if it wasn't meant to be, you wouldn't have been on Facebook and I wouldn't have been able to find you.'

Petula giggled.

'I knew I could make you smile.'

'You know, maybe it's not completely accurate that I forgot about you. What I do remember is that sense of humour. You could always make me smile, Glen.'

'So, you did miss me. You did think about me, at least sometimes.'

'But I left you... I broke your heart. Why would you care about me?'

Glen thought for a moment. 'You know, I'm not sure. I should have hated you, but I didn't. For some reason you've been on my mind all these years.'

'I left you for another man.'

'You made a mistake.'

'I've made lots of mistakes. If I told you, you'd leave me. So I'd have to keep them secret and they'd fester; we'd end up hating each other—is that what you want?'

'So tell me. Tell me all your mistakes and I'll tell you mine.'

'Why?'

'Because I've wasted too much time. I should have looked for you years ago.'

'Okay.' She took a deep breath. 'I *was* a drug addict, and I used to shoplift to feed my habit. I spent a week in jail not so long ago. I live in a housing association flat, and the temptation to take drugs is all around me there and I'm not

so sure I'll be able to resist for ever. I live from day to day.'
She looked around after her mini-speech as if worried in case
anyone had heard.

Glen noticed a young couple were walking towards
them, eyes trained on their smartphones; it was unlikely they
would have been listening in to his and Petula's conversation.
Besides, in the age of so much information being available in
the public realm, in this world overrun with technology, with
every little secret of people's lives laid bare and open on
Facebook, it was doubtful passersby would be shocked by her
revelations.

He looked at her standing there now with a dejected
frown on her face. He did feel shocked by what he'd heard
but somehow he could only feel a sense of sorrow and
sympathy. Sorrow for the years that had passed between
them, and sympathy for what she had been through.
Something told him that if she hadn't taken the wrong turn
and left him back then, both of their lives would have been
much easier. He felt the burden of partial responsibility as
well because he had been so out of touch in those days. He'd
taken her for granted.

'So now you know,' she said, her cheeks flushed.
'Thank you for everything, Glen. I think you were a lifeline
without knowing it. When you got in touch again and said
you wanted to see me, it motivated me to look for work, to do
my hair, and get some new clothes. All this is down to you.'
She puffed up her hair with her hands. 'If you'd seen me
before, you'd have run a mile. Thanks for helping. I think I'll
be fine now. I don't expect you to stay. You're too good for
me. Leave now before I have the chance to destroy you. I
destroy everything I touch.'

'You're too hard on yourself. I don't care about the
past. All I see when I look at you is Petula Harrigan, the girl
I've always loved.'

'You're living in a dream world.'

'Maybe I am. The question is, would you like to join me there?'

He held out his hand and she took hold of it, tears in her eyes.

Chapter Forty-Three

'I've packed your suitcase,' said George as soon as Belinda sauntered in through the front door the following morning.

She looked at him and then at the black suitcase on the floor in front of her.

George watched as her eyes drifted to the boxes he'd placed in the hallway.

After closing the door behind her, she walked towards him and gave him a peck on the cheek. 'I didn't know the completion was today. Isn't it next week?'

'It is next week,' said George, his arms folded, a deep frown on his face.

'So, why have you packed my bags? I'll need stuff from in there.' She giggled.

'It's over, Belinda. I'm not part of your little game anymore, and—more importantly—I don't want you anywhere near my son.'

She stared at him, her mouth opening and closing like that of a fish a couple of times, no sound coming out.

'I know all about you and Fernando. And I know you think I'm a creep and a loser. I heard you yesterday.'

'You were at the pub... You-you followed me? You are sick, do you know that? You're a—'

'Get out!'

'For your information, old man, I was never interested in you, I only wanted the money. No one would be interested in you. No wonder your wife left you; you're crap in bed. So boring. I'm happy to leave, and I feel sorry for your son, but he'll probably end up like you. Like father, like son.' She grabbed her suitcase with a shaky hand and opened the front door. 'Have a nice life, George.'

The door slammed behind her, and although he tried

to tell himself that what she'd just said had been fuelled by anger and by the humiliation of being found out, each and every one of her words resounded in his head. *Old man. So boring. No wonder your wife left you. You're crap in bed. Old man. I was never interested in you. So boring. Old man.*

Part of him felt proud that he'd stood up for himself, but the greater part felt broken and alone. More alone than ever.

Unable to see a road ahead, just more road blocks, he sat on the floor next to the removal boxes. Now he was being forced to leave this house—the house he'd worked so hard for; the house he loved. All because his wife left him. None of it was his fault, yet he'd ended up paying. How was that fair? Where would he be living come next week? Half the money from the house sale would go to Roisin, and the other half wasn't sufficient for a deposit on a house so he'd have to rent; rental properties in the area were expensive, but it had to be local so Robbie could stay with him during the week. Problem after problem seemed to be piling up on top of him. He put his head in his hands and wept.

His mobile sounded to let him know he'd received a text. Probably Belinda with more caustic remarks. He hesitated before looking at the phone. Tom's name was showing on the display.

He clicked through to his inbox and read the text message:

Jess found out where to get what you asked for. They'll deliver to your house in a couple of days.

His eyes remained fixed on the message for a short time. A small lifeline. Perhaps after he'd taken the spider to the house, Rex would leave him alone. He tried to look at the positive side: soon, he and Robbie would be living in another house, somewhere without any ghosts attached. They'd be starting again. Everything was slipping back to some kind of normality.

The doorbell rang and he expected it was Belinda returning for something. He grabbed a tissue and wiped his eyes, checking his reflection in the hallway mirror, not wanting to give her the satisfaction of thinking she had upset him with her words.

Cursing, he stomped to the door and opened it aggressively.

Robbie stood in the doorway, his overnight bag by his side.

George quickly changed his scowl to a smile and greeted his father, who had brought Robbie home.

'Hello, George.'

'Thanks for bringing him back, Dad. I would have come—'

'No, it's all right. Your mother was worried he might be late for school, so I thought I'd bring him, save you the journey; I know you have to work.'

'Thanks.'

'He's had breakfast, so he should be ready for school.'

'Great.'

'I'll get my book-bag,' said Robbie.

George looked at his watch. 'It's still early, son; go and watch some TV. Do you want to come in, Dad?'

'I know you're busy, but yes, I will just for a minute if that's all right. Something Robbie said has been bothering me.'

'Come in,' said George, feeling deflated, knowing that Robbie must have talked about Roisin leaving home.

'What are these boxes?' asked George's dad as he made his way to the living room.

'Um... I'm sure I told you we're selling the house,' said George, knowing he hadn't told his parents anything, unable to find a way to break the news to them. They were fond of Roisin.

His dad sat on the sofa and removed his hat, a brown flat cap.

George sat next to him.

'I'll get straight to the point because I know you have to take the boy to school. Have you and Roisin split up?'

George searched his father's expression to try to garner what his reaction would be to the news.

'I-I was going to tell you.'

'Don't worry, son, it's not uncommon these days. All your mother and I wanted to do was let you know that we're here if you need us. You know, helping with Robbie and such things.'

'That's... um... That's kind. I didn't know how you'd take the news... Didn't want to worry you.'

'We were upset when we heard. I like Roisin, your mother does too. She's a good influence on Robbie. I assume you will have worked out arrangements for where he'll be staying. He will be staying with you, won't he?'

'I hope so.' George covered his face with his hands momentarily. Not having expected to have to talk about this with his father, he felt pressured. 'I-I, she had an affair. She's pregnant again, but it's not my child. She's living with the father. I'm selling this house to pay back the money she put in. I didn't want to move, but I think I need a fresh start.'

'I think you're right. I'm sure there are lots of memories in this house.'

'Yes.'

His father put on his hat. 'I won't keep you; just wanted to make sure you're all right.'

'Thanks, Dad.' George followed him to the front door.

Chapter Forty-Four

The package was delivered on Saturday morning.

The man parked a white van by the side of the road, stepped out carrying a brown parcel that could have contained anything, and walked towards George's house.

George had just returned from taking Robbie to Roisin's parents' house. The delivery man caught him as he opened the front door.

'Hello,' said George.

The man's facial expression remained fixed. 'Good morning, sir,' he said, and tipped his hat before handing over the parcel. 'Please make sure you don't tell anyone where you got this.'

'I-I won't,' said George, feeling slightly threatened by the man's demeanour.

'Good day, sir.'

'Er... thank you. Um... Do you want me to pay you?'

'No, the boss will sort it out. You'll be hearing from him.'

George nodded and watched the man leave. *"The boss"*; the way the man had said it brought to mind images of mafia bosses from old movies. He prayed he hadn't got himself into something illegal that might have repercussions.

As if suddenly waking up to the fact that the package he held contained a poisonous spider, George ran into the living room and placed it on the coffee table. There were small holes—tiny, practically invisible—dotted around the package; ventilation for the spider. What if the deadly creature escaped through one of the holes? Maybe it would see a tiny spot of daylight and use its teeth to free itself. Did spiders have teeth? Fangs? George shivered at the thought. One thing he did know was that he wouldn't feel comfortable leaving the package here all day. He'd planned to deliver it to 8 Goldfern Road in the night, under cover of darkness.

Contemplating this, the thought occurred to him that he didn't even know if the house had been sold yet. It was probably still on the market, though, following the spider incident when the would-be purchasers were scared away. Roisin had called him again later that day, ranting down the phone about how he'd have to pay for the pest control company who were attending to kill the spiders.

He'd reacted by swearing at her and saying, 'It's your problem. It's nothing to do with me.'

The familiar dark cloud descended as he realised that until the spider was delivered, Rex remained a thorn in his side.

George felt fearful of taking the spider to the house. There were a number of potential accidents waiting to happen. Firstly, what if someone saw him putting the spider through the letterbox? Secondly, opening the parcel frightened him; the spider might escape. Also, what would happen if the spider somehow got out and he had to handle it? If it bit him, he'd die. Jess had said it was a Brazilian spider, thought to be the most venomous species in the world.

Lifting the package, he could feel the creature moving around inside; it would be agitated, and angry about being trapped for so long. What if it attacked as soon as released?

George's anxiety was building, along with a sense of urgency to be rid of the creature.

Negative thoughts clouded his brain as he got into his car; his hands shook and he worried he'd have an accident on the way to the house.

'I hope you're satisfied, Rex,' he mumbled under his breath, as he fastened his seatbelt.

The package sat on the front passenger seat of his car.

There was something eerie about the presence of a deadly spider in the car. Rex may have planned this all along, knowing full well that any poisonous spider would kill George before he had the chance to deliver it; after all, *The Spider*'s mission had been to "destroy" George. Why would that have changed?

He started the engine with terror in his heart.

🕷

'Hurry up, Roisin, we have to leave,' said Hugh.

They were getting ready to visit the house at 8 Goldfern Road. The estate agent had found them a buyer from overseas keen for a quick exchange and completion: he planned to use the property as an investment and didn't want to miss out on any rental income; there was a tenant lined up and ready to move in.

Hugh and Roisin were having a meeting with the agent and their solicitor at the property so they could sign the contracts. Everything was rushed because they didn't want to lose the buyer.

George had dropped Robbie off for his weekend stay half an hour ago. As soon as the boy arrived he said he had a tummy ache and wanted to lie down.

'Hugh!' Roisin called from the room where Robbie slept, 'Do I have to come? Robbie's not well.'

Roisin and Hugh were still lodging with her parents until the house sale completed. Her parents were out at a local church meeting.

'He'll be fine here on his own, won't he?' called Hugh.

'No, I'm not leaving him.'

Hugh rushed up the stairs. 'I'll carry him and we'll put him in the back of the car.'

'Okay,' said Roisin, wearing a worried frown.

Once Robbie was safely fastened in, Roisin climbed into the passenger seat.

Hugh got into the car and smiled at her. 'It's all working out perfectly,' he said. 'The house'll be sold before we know it, and the baby will be born just in time to move into our new place.'

'I hope so,' she said, twisting around to try to look at Robbie, but it was too uncomfortable so she stared straight out of the windscreen. She wondered, not for the first time, whether Robbie was feeling ill because he knew that soon she'd have another child and that, in a way, he was being replaced, especially as he didn't see her often.

'Do you think I'm a bad mother?' she asked, speaking her thoughts.

'You're the best mother, Roisin. Isn't that right, Robbie?' Hugh started the engine and pulled away from the kerb.

Robbie didn't reply, and Roisin hoped he might be sleeping, not just evading the question. 'Robbie darling, when we get the new house, you'll be coming to stay with us and your little sister, okay?'

'I don't want a little sister,' grumbled Robbie.

Hugh touched her hand. 'Don't worry, when she arrives he'll fall in love with her; you'll see.'

George's breath came in short gasps as he opened the package that contained the deadly spider. He took a deep breath, relieved when he found a plastic container inside with the spider safely enclosed within it.

He was leaning down next to the letterbox at 8 Goldfern Road. He'd done his best to make sure no one saw him enter the gate. The street was never very busy, being made up of residential houses and situated away from the main high road. There were hardly any moving cars, or people around when he'd arrived. He had rushed to get to the door before anyone saw him.

He lined the plastic container up with the letter box, then he carefully placed his hand on the edge of the container and pulled the lid away to enable the spider to get out.

To his surprise, the spider moved quickly when the lid opened, and it ran straight through the letterbox. George pulled the empty container away and his heartbeat slowly returned to normal.

'Goodbye, Rex,' he said as he rushed back to his car and set off at speed towards the high street.

As he turned the corner of the street, he was sure he heard Rex laughing.

Rex hovered above the spider as it crawled into the living room of 8 Goldfern Road. *'Such a beautiful specimen,'* he said. *'A Brazilian wandering spider, if I'm not mistaken.'*

He moved in closer to look at the object of his desire. *'You could kill a man with one bite. Excellent. George, you have excelled yourself. All is forgiven. Now I will reign supreme in this house. No one will enter without paying the price. I am the winner.'*

A raucous laugh shattered the silence as Rex swooped down and possessed the body of the spider.

Hugh, Roisin, and Robbie arrived at the house after a twenty-minute drive.

As Roisin stepped out of the car she was sure she saw George's car turn the corner of the street, but it had gone now and she couldn't be certain. She opened the back door of the car. 'Come on, Robbie.'

Robbie jumped out, and ran to the front door of the house. 'Is this our new house?' he asked when Roisin and Hugh caught up with him.

'No, darling. We're selling this one.'

'But I like this one,' said Robbie.

'The new one is even better, Robbie,' said Hugh. He stepped onto the doorstep and unlocked the door.

Robbie ran inside.

'I'll just make sure everything's in order,' said Roisin. 'I don't want any surprises after the last time.' She made her way through to the kitchen.

Hugh shouted out, 'I'll check upstairs.'

A few minutes later, Hugh made his way down to the hallway and Robbie grabbed his leg. 'Hugh, Hugh, there's a spider in there!'

'Oh, no! Not more spiders!'

'Spiders?' Roisin came running from the kitchen. 'Oh, my God! How many this time?'

'Only one, Mummy, but it's scary.' Robbie began to weep.

'Hey, Robbie, don't worry, show me where it is,' said Hugh, picking up the boy and walking into the living room.

'There! There!' screamed Robbie.

Hugh laughed. 'That little thing?' Then he called back to Roisin, 'Don't worry, honey, it's only one house spider. I'll get rid of it.'

'Will you kill it, Hugh? Please.' Robbie clung on to him tightly.

'Go to your mother, Robbie, and I'll get rid of it.' He took the boy into the hallway and released him from his hold.

My first victim, thought Rex, looking up to see a tall man enter the room. His adrenaline rush turned to fear as darkness appeared to descend almost instantaneously.

Hugh stomped on the spider with his cowboy boot. There was a crunching sound and he pressed his foot down hard just to make sure it was dead.

www.ingramcontent.com/pod-product-compliance
Lightning Source LLC
Chambersburg PA
CBHW051634260626
47170CB00004B/1180